The Antique Picker's Daughter

The publisher gratefully acknowledges the support of the Canada Council for the Arts, Ontario Arts Council, Ontario Creates and the Canadian Government.

Cover design: Juliane Van Huizen

Canada Council for the Arts | Conseil des arts du Canada

ONTARIO CREATES

ONTARIO ARTS COUNCIL
CONSEIL DES ARTS DE L'ONTARIO
an Ontario government agency
un organisme du gouvernement de l'Ontario

Canada

Library and Archives Canada Cataloguing in Publication

Title: The antique picker's daughter / Melanie Dugan.

Names: Dugan, Melanie, author.

Series: Inanna poetry & fiction series.

Description: Series statement: Inanna poetry and fiction series

Identifiers: Canadiana (print) 20260240184 | Canadiana (ebook) 20260240206 | ISBN 9781834210322 (softcover) | ISBN 9781834210339 (EPUB) | ISBN 9781834210575 (PDF) Subjects: LCGFT: Novels.

Classification: LCC PS8557.U3214 A83 2026 | DDC C813/.6—dc23

INANNA
PUBLICATIONS & EDUCATION INC.
TORONTO, ONTARIO, CANADA
www.inanna.ca

Printed and bound in Canada

Inanna Publications and Education Inc.

210 Founders College, York University

4700 Keele Street, Toronto, Ontario, Canada M3J 1P3

Telephone: (416) 736-5356 Fax: (416) 736-5765

Email: inanna.publications@inanna.ca

Website: www.inanna.ca

The Antique Picker's Daughter

a novel

Melanie Dugan

For S.T.

Table of Contents

1. The Beginning

1.

THE FIRST THING YOU NEED TO KNOW: They're not antiques.

The second thing: I'm not his daughter.

My name is Frances Person. Not my real name, not the name my parents gave me—about the only thing my father was involved in giving me. And since I don't want any souvenirs of him, when Francis said in a teasing tone, "You'll be Frances Person, just so everyone knows you're a person." I said, "Okay." It was that easy to become someone else. Or to become my real self. One or the other, I'm not sure which.

He told me his name is Francis Person. It may be his real name, I doubt it. So, he's Francis and I'm Frances—names that look different but sound identical. A daughter named after her father makes sense to them; the marks, the stiffs, the toffs, as he calls the people we buy from and sell to. Our similar names emphasize the connection between him and me. And it helps that we resemble each other: both of us sandy-haired with grey-green eyes, both wiry and thin.

When it's just us, he calls me Frankie.

Francis and Frankie.

A lot of the time they're not real antiques, the articles we buy—or otherwise acquire—but they seem like they are, or could be. Francis says about the clients, "If they don't ask, we won't tell them. It's not our fault if there's some misperception at their end." This is his way of talking, the big words. "You'll thank me later," he says, "for expanding your vocabulary." He's always reading books as we travel around, books on clouds, economics, history, any number of subjects. "Esoterica," he calls it. I call it a bunch of useless information. He says he's an "autodidact," whatever that means. "Look it up in the dictionary," he tells me.

I say, "Buy me one at the next market."

He has an expert eye. He knows Chippendale from Hepplewhite (not hard – I prefer Hepplewhite, less fussy). More to the point, he can tell real Chippendale from fake (one way to tell them apart, he has taught me, is the fake pieces often appear to be older than the real ones), authentic Tiffany (which he says is sentimental crap, and the people who want to buy it deserve a lesson) from a copy. That's what really matters, he says; the customers may not be able to tell the difference, but we need to be able to. Sell them the genuine article? For the pittance we ask? It'd be a crime, theft, he says. Except we'd be stealing from ourselves, and only fools and saints do that.

"I'm not a saint," Francis says, "but I'm not a fool, either."

That's one of the differences between us and the clients, he says: we have to be professionals. A few months after I started travelling with him, we were at a flea market near Owen Sound, I think it was. I was doing the once-around when suddenly he appeared beside me. This never happened—the rule was, we each did the once-around and then we'd rendezvous off-site, away from the market, church basement, or community centre the sale was at. But this time he simply appeared right beside me—poof!—out of thin air. I was surprised, and stared at him.

"Look," he said. I could hear the thrill in his voice. He was holding what looked like an old glass bottle, dark blue. Nothing to get excited about as far as I could see. "It's the real McCoy," he said in a hushed tone. "A Hutchinson Bottle—a Hutch."

"Yeah? So?" It was a glass bottle. No big deal.

He let out an exasperated breath. "You don't see many of these in such excellent shape—and cobalt blue? That's rare. Fortunately," he lowered his voice, "the folks selling this had no idea what it was worth. That's the difference between amateurs and professionals. Professionals know what's real and what's fake. Professionals know the true value of the items in their possession. Amateurs? Well, *pffft*. To quote someone—I can't recall who—amateurs know the price of everything, and the value of nothing."

Then he launched into a disquisition on all the different types of glass bottles I should be keeping my eyes open for: Hutches, Roonboroughs, Gothic bottles, Cathedral bottles, blob tops, stoppered, salt glazed, milk, soda, perfume. I thought my ears would fall off.

~

Here's how it works; Francis and me, we keep to the back roads most of the time, driving along in his old pickup. He sits behind the wheel, and between us on the seat is a wall of items: on his side are the *tome* he's currently reading, a toolbox for when the truck is what he calls *recalcitrant*, and pamphlets and brochures collected for background information. In the middle are paper bags with our most recent on-the-run meal. On my side are books I read when the drive is long, some novels but mostly non-fiction, and a few magazines about antiques and collectibles (he says I need a wide range of knowledge to be really useful).

He built this wall: he keeps it there, and if any of my bits or pieces ever slip onto his side of the seat, he pushes them back and says, "You keep your stuff on your side, Missy. Your property is your property, mine is mine, and never the twain shall meet." Which sounds like another quote.

There's a bubble around him I'm always on the outside of. I'm okay with that. In my experience, people you get close to don't always stick around. Maybe keeping a distance is better for things to work out over the long run.

Jammed into the space behind the seat is his bag and my knapsack, carrying our clothes, toothbrushes, and other necessities.

The truck is rusty, but not too rusty. We don't want to stand out, he says. His custom-made trailer is hitched up behind, full of miscellaneous objects. It's roomy, the trailer, like the ones plumbers and carpenters haul around. You can stand up in it. "Inventory," he calls what's inside the trailer; junk is what I call it.

"Now, now," he says, right hand on the steering wheel, left arm dangling out the window. "Beauty is in the eye of the beholder. If someone wants an item, it's beautiful in their eyes, a treasure. We simply help them see the object's inner beauty. We help them understand exactly how much they want it."

~

Francis has an eye not only for inventory but also for opportunity. Every barn we pass is a possible gold mine; filled to the rafters, perhaps, with old furniture, antique canoes, ancient farm machinery, all sorts of articles and items that might be treasures. Even planks of barn board have potential. "There's folks that love to stick that up on their rec room walls. Makes them feel all rustic," he says with a sarcastic curl to his mouth.

He's not above just turning off a main road and bumping along rutted tracks that serve as a driveway to knock on someone's door and ask to see their barn. I always half-expect he'll have the door slammed in his face or get popped by a farmer angry at strangers showing up and asking for a tour, but it never happens. Francis has this bottomless well of charm. Men and women alike fall under his spell, open their doors, invite him in. They offer him (us) coffee, tea, cookies, sandwiches. Then they lead us out to their barn or up to their attic.

Here's how it often went—this was a while ago, in June, I think: the days were warming up, and we'd seen one or two flocks of geese far up in the sky heading north. We were out on some concession road. The last town we'd stopped in was Shelburne. The week before we'd been further north, maybe around Bracebridge, I'm not entirely sure. The land here was flatter, with fewer trees. You could see farther—there were what Francis called *vistas*, where the land unrolled off to the horizon.

We were cruising along, not in any hurry. Inventory was low, and he was on the look-out for what he called "infusions of merchandise."

Off to the right he spotted a farm with a small, run down-looking house, its paint peeling off the clapboard, the front yard overrun with violets, white Queen Anne's Lace, and yellow dandelions ("While you're educating yourself, it wouldn't hurt you to learn some botany," he said once, pushing a book at me on Southern Ontario flora and fauna he'd picked up at the last market). Beside the house sat a barn with a sagging roof and empty black spaces in the walls, like teeth missing in someone's smile, where planks had disappeared.

"Well, Frankie," he said, "there you have it: your classic dump." The first time he said something along these lines, I was sort of offended for the people he was talking about, but now I've spent time with him I know this is how he talks: a little dramatic and sort of funny, a bit mean sometimes. "Probably nothing there for us, but it doesn't cost a thing to take a look. It can be a profitable day when people have an item or two they don't know the real value of."

He eased up on the gas and turned off the highway onto a pot-holed road. We rattled along it until we came to the driveway where we turned in, gravel tinging against the bottom of the truck.

When we were near the house, he slowed down. Francis is always on the look-out for dogs. Most dogs he's okay with. He keeps a bag of liver treats in the glove compartment, and if dogs come bounding up to the truck, he'll grab a few before he gets out. He can usually distract them with the treats. But with some dogs, he stops the truck, turns around, and drives back the way we came. "No point in risking life and limb for some cheesy knickknack," he says.

This time there were no dogs. He stopped a fair distance from the front door of the house. It made people nervous, he said, if we got up close and personal too quick.

He climbed out of the truck and stretched as if his back was stiff, even though we'd only been on the road about half an hour by that time. It was a performance, one that offered him a chance to give the place a quick once-over before proceeding. After a second, he straightened, scratched the back of his head, leaned in the driver's side and said, "Come on."

I didn't like these cold calls. It made me nervous to go up to a stranger's house and bang on the door or ring the doorbell, but Francis said, "If you don't go treasure hunting, you'll never find any treasure. They can say no, but they might say yes. Sometimes you have to get through no to get to yes. And you have to learn how to do this, Frankie. I'm not always going to be around." As if this was what I'd be doing for the rest of my life. I didn't tell him I wasn't planning on continuing in this field, this business wasn't my future. I simply climbed out and followed him.

Across the path leading up to the house stood a chain-link fence with a gate in the middle of it. The fence wasn't very long, maybe four meters wide, and didn't really seem to serve any purpose; it wasn't part of a larger fence around the property, it just stood there all alone, blocking the path to the house. On one side it stopped at the edge of the driveway, and on the other side it just stopped. I mean, you could walk around either end of it and on up to the house, but for some reason they'd built a fence blocking the path and put a gate in the middle of it. So, Francis opened the gate and we went up to the side door. He knocked and waited, glancing over at me.

Nothing happened. Francis rocked back and forth on his heels, stuck his hands in his pockets, and looked around in a random way, all loose and casual. I thought he was about to give up and walk back to the truck when the door swung open and a man glared out at us. He was older, maybe in his sixties, short and skinny except for a small, round belly bracketed by suspenders that stuck out over the waistband of his trousers. He had wispy white hair, surprisingly unwrinkled skin, and eyes like a crow's: shiny black buttons, glittering and sharp. He didn't say anything, simply fixed those bright eyes on Francis.

"Hi," Francis said. He'd adopted a low-key, drawling tone. "I'm Roy and this is my daughter Sue-Ellen." He tilted his head in my direction, keeping a careful distance between him and me.

("Give them my real name?" he said to me early on. "About as likely as me telling them how much their Aunt Nancy's Wedgwood sugar bowl is really worth.")

The man's gaze tracked from Francis to me and back.

This was how we played it. Francis said it would be weird in a bad way if I was travelling around with an older man who wasn't my father. "People might get bent out of shape about it," he said.

"My business is collectibles," Francis continued. He paused to let his words sink in. "Nothing fancy—that's not my snack bracket. I'm after, you know, small things—vintage mementoes, doodads, oldie goldies I can sell at the flea market." The man was still staring, but he hadn't shut the door. ("As long as the door's still open, we're halfway to yes," was one of Francis's aphorisms. He told me once, "I'm full of aphorisms." He glanced at me, read my expression. "I know what you're thinking—you're thinking I'm full of something else. None of that sauciness, Missy.")

"Me and Sue-Ellen, we're driving along and see your charming place—" here Francis beamed, his eyes crinkling at the corners "—and I noticed that barn of yours." He jerked his thumb in the direction of the pile. "And I said to Sue-Ellen, you know, maybe there're treasures in there. You never can tell." He raised his eyebrows, as if he and the guy were sharing a secret. "Like I tell Sue-Ellen, people don't always know when they have articles of real value." What he was saying was a spin on his real opinions. Francis says the closer to the truth you can stick, the more believable you'll sound. Believable is a big weapon in our armoury, I have learned.

The man's crow's eyes narrowed warily.

"Maybe I could have a look-see, maybe take some items off your hands for cash?"

For a second I watched, as first curiosity and then caution flickered across the man's face. After a minute he stepped out of his house and pulled the door shut. He looked Francis up and down. Then he said, "Sure," in an oddly reedy voice.

"Great!" said Francis, all enthusiasm. "Sweet place you have here. I tell Sue-Ellen, when I retire—*if* I retire—" he added with a rueful chuckle,"—this is exactly the type of place I'll be looking for: quiet, surrounded by beautiful country. You have it made in the shade here."

The man didn't reply, just led us up the barn's ramp. At the top, he tugged the door sideways; it groaned and only opened partway because the barn had settled and the doorframe was off plumb. "The name's Horace," he said, stepping through. We followed him into the darkness.

The air in the barn was thick and still. It smelled of dust and straw and old manure. There were some bales stacked in disorderly piles, but most of the space was taken up by old furniture and cardboard boxes. The furniture was scruffy and worn, covered in nubby plaid fabric, 1970s vintage, I'd guess—you spend time with Francis, you pick up this kind of information. The boxes were lying around randomly, a lot of them half-open, as if someone had gone digging through them at one point and then had walked off and left them. They held odds and ends from what I could see, junk, mostly, chipped coffee mugs with silly mottoes or ugly pictures, stained rag rugs, old paperback novels I knew would smell of mildew. There were bird droppings everywhere, clumps of straw scattered all over. The place depressed me; these stained, smelly odds and ends were someone's memories—or a few people's—covered in dust and bits of straw and bird poo, smelling slightly of manure and mildew because they'd been stored here so long.

"There's this—" Horace had bent over one of the open boxes, now he stood up and brandished what looked like a round, black cookie tin, old and dented, the paint rubbed off in places so the silver of the tin showed through—"my grandmother's button box."

Francis glanced at me. I knew what he was thinking: *Buttons?*

"I've never had much luck with buttons," he said.

Horace dipped into another box. "This was my grandfather's, from the First War." He held up a shallow, saucer-shaped helmet.

"I know a guy who deals in that stuff. I'll send him your way," Francis said. From the tone of his voice, I knew he didn't know anyone like that, there was no one he would send Horace's way. "But war memorabilia doesn't move too well for me."

Francis didn't let on, but I could tell the place was a disappointment. The sparkle in his smile dimmed, the twinkle in his eyes flickered, his patter slowed. We stood in the space as dust motes silted down rays of light angling through the gaps in the walls while Horace pulled one tattered item after another out of various boxes. Each new object, Francis nodded with a little less energy, agreed a little less enthusiastically with Horace's comments. In the end he pulled out his wallet and handed Horace twenty dollars for six Canadian swirl tumblers.

We left the barn and Francis made a big deal of getting Horace's phone number for the guy who might be interested in the helmet—the guy who would never call. By this time Horace and Francis were friends. They shook hands. Horace stood in the driveway and waved as we pulled away.

Afterwards, back on the road, Francis shook his head. "What a pile of garbage. That place is a fire hazard." I could tell he was disappointed. It made him cranky.

~

But sometimes, he hits pay dirt. Depending on our current level of liquidity, as he puts it, he takes as much as he can fit into the trailer. If we're already pretty full up, he'll pick only the best items, but he scribbles a note about the place, the address or location, in a notebook he keeps in a pocket of his jacket so we can come back at a later date.

He offers the owner a good deal—these people aren't stupid—but never a great one, never too good. He says they don't need to know how valuable Aunt May's breakfront china case with leaded, etched glass windows really is, or the true worth of the pure oak wainscoting someone dumped in the barn when they put up the new fiberboard garbage. Plus, he knows most of the time they'll try to dicker him up, so he starts low. Once in a while he'll go higher—the antique rocking chair he knew was what he called "the real McCoy," although it looked rickety and uncomfortable to me and I told him so, and another time a cherrywood table clock; he has a soft spot for cherrywood. Those are the times he'll go slightly higher than he planned—it doesn't happen often. "We're working on a budget," he says. "A penny saved and all that."

As I said, he has charm and can cast his spell over pretty much everyone. Everyone except me. I'm immune, I guess. I don't know why, but his charm doesn't work on me. He knows it, but he forgets sometimes and starts gearing up. He can't help it, I figure. His charm is a reflex or an instinct, automatic. When he's getting started, his eyes crinkle and he gets playful. Usually, it's when he wants me to do something he knows I won't want to do, like tell a fib or distract someone—when he's trying to use me as his secret weapon. "Hey, Frankie," he'll say in a low voice, like we share a secret, trying to soften me up.

Then I fix him with my look, the *don't fuck with me* look I worked up in the tough times before I met him, and I say, "Don't start."

His grin dissolves and fades. Puzzlement flickers across his face. As I watch, an internal struggle goes on. A faint frown tightens his forehead and after a second, I see understanding dawn: He was going to try and con *me*. He shakes his head and laughs. "You're a hard woman, Frankie."

"I'd better be," I tell him. "Spending this much time with someone like you. You'd con your mother if you thought you could make a penny out of it."

He looks hurt, shakes his head. "That's hard. So young and so hard-hearted."

"Tell me it isn't true, then."

He gives a tiny shrug. "Well, not for a penny, anyhow."

2.

WHEN I FIRST MET HIM, I was on the street. It was cold and getting colder. The day we met, I wasn't sure where I was going to stay that night. My gut was a tight knot of worry. My plan was to keep moving around and try to sleep in the library the next day. They don't like you doing that, though. They come around and wake you up. They're not supposed to touch you so they stand beside you and cough, say, "Excuse me," and then explain you can't sleep there. But sometimes if you're deep asleep, they have to nudge you gently with their foot, and afterwards they apologize.

I was downtown, waiting on the sidewalk in front of the Eaton Centre, near one of the entrances. A door would open and you'd get a blast of warm air. Once in a while I'd go inside to get out of the cold, but security would come along pretty quickly and tell me to move on, which meant move outside. What was I waiting for out on the sidewalk? That was the question.

I was standing by the door, and Francis comes up to me and says, "You look cold." Yeah, I was freezing. I'd left my gran's house getting on a month earlier with only the clothes on my back and all the cash I could find in the house. Now I was almost out of money. I hadn't eaten a real meal in a few days. I hadn't taken a shower for a while and my clothes were gross, damp and slightly sticky the way they get when you've worn them a long time. I was tired, the way you get when you're living like that—having to keep your eyes open all the time and stay alert—tired in your whole body, achy.

"You want a coffee?" he asked.

He was tall and slim with collar-length dirty blond hair that had a touch of grey at the temples, hazel-coloured eyes, and an open, friendly manner. I figured he was old enough to be my dad. Not that I had a lot of experience in this area, my dad having taken off a couple of years after I arrived, but this guy looked about the age my dad could have been.

I'd always been what my gran called "an observer." Mostly, I think, because of Mom and me bouncing around a lot. I learned to keep my eyes open and my mouth shut. Once I started living on the street, I began watching people even more closely. You have to. If you don't, before you know it, someone'll be selling you your own clothes, the ones they've lifted off your back when you were distracted—probably by a friend of theirs.

This guy was dressed sort of country: jeans, a denim jacket, cowboy boots—but they weren't nose pickers, they were scuffed and scratched like real work boots would be.

His voice was low. The way he talked, it sounded like we were on a team, only the two of us and no one else, that we shared an understanding of some sort. I couldn't tell how he did it. But there was a sadness about him, too, the way his smile stopped before it made it all the way up to his eyes.

Was he hitting on me? By then I had some experience with this. I'd had guys come on to me, and I'd heard from other girls how it worked. A guy acting concerned, helpful, offering them food, a place to crash, and the next thing, he's beaten them up and they're on the street working for him. And he says if she tries to get away, he'll find her and finish the job.

I'd had a few guys try this. They'd materialize beside me suddenly, really friendly and sympathetic, asking, "How you doing?" as if they were genuinely concerned about me. One guy, older, near the library as I left one day, calling, "Hi, how are you?" all upbeat and cheerful. But I could sense an edgy, tingling, uncomfortable current beneath his words, and I knew enough to know he couldn't care less about how I was, so I told him to fuck off.

A quick flash of suspicion must have slipped across my face with the guy who'd offered me a coffee. "No, no, nothing like that," he said. He held up one hand and stepped back, putting more distance between us. "You remind me of my daughter is all."

I rolled my eyes. He pulled out his wallet, the leather worn and shiny from use, and slipped out a photo. It had been cut from one of those strips, four in a row, from a booth in the mall. He handed it to me, a picture of a pretty girl, prettier than me, with long, blonde hair, beaming as if life was so great it couldn't get any better. She looked sort of like him around the eyes. The photo was in rough shape, one corner had been folded so there was a white line running through the top left side of her hair, and the edges were soft from being handled a lot. I turned it over. "Phoebe" was written in pencil on the back, so faded it had almost disappeared. He'd been carrying that picture around a long time.

The careful way he pulled it out, the way his expression softened when he looked at it before passing it to me, I could tell he was proud of her. I didn't figure anyone had ever looked at a picture of me that way.

"Her name's Phoebe," he said. "My name's Francis."

I handed the picture back. "Just a coffee," I said, even though I was hungry. I hadn't eaten since some lady handed me a bag of donut holes early that morning. I'd been sitting in a bus shelter to get out of the wind, and she'd been on her way to work, it looked like. She was dressed for the office, a long navy-blue coat, fashionable shiny black boots, expensive haircut. I saw her eyes snag on me when she came into the shelter, then she turned and left. *Oh, God*, I thought, *she's going to tell a cop, and he'll come and make me move along.* I considered getting up and leaving, but I was tired and I figured I'd stay put as long as I could, keep warm a few minutes longer. The next I know, she's back, pushing a bag of donut holes into my hand.

I looked at her. "Thanks," I said. Usually, people ignored me or glared at me. It looked like she was about to say something, but then she turned and walked away. So, when Francis said, "Coffee," I was hollow from hunger. The whole middle of me was a burning ache.

"Sure, just a coffee," he said. There was a Tim Horton's on the corner. He walked towards it and I followed him. A guy came out when we were close, and the sugary smell drifting out with him hit me so hard I thought I'd collapse right there on the sidewalk. You can know you're hungry, but it's not until you see or smell something good to eat that it hits you how hungry you are, how empty inside.

Inside the Timmie's Francis said, "Grab us a table."

I went and sat at one right in the middle of the room with a clear path to the door so if he tried anything creepy there'd be witnesses, and I could get away fast if I needed to.

But nothing strange happened. He came back with two coffees and two bowls of soup. "I'm having a bite to eat," he said. "Thought you might like some, too." A small bread roll came with each bowl of soup. He pushed his roll over to me. "Middle-age spread," he patted his stomach. "I don't need that."

We ate for a while. Then he said, "Pheebes was seventeen her last birthday. How old are you?"

"Sixteen," I told him. I was a few months short of it—well, almost a year short of it.

He smiled at me, the ghost of a smile, that said *I know you're lying, and you know I know.*

"Next birthday," I added.

"I'd hate to see Pheebes on the street." He said this thoughtfully and let the words hang there between us.

I was trying not to eat too fast. I'd done that before. After the first few days, when I saw how quickly money evaporated, I decided I could afford one real meal a day. I'd have coffees through the day, maybe a donut or cookies, and get a substantial meal for supper. Then one day I'd found a twenty-dollar bill in a book at the library. Imagine using a twenty-dollar bill as a bookmark? I went to McDonald's and bought two quarter-pounders, plus fries and a drink, and wolfed it all down. It felt great at first, but I threw it all up later.

"Who says I'm on the street?" I demanded.

Francis just looked at me.

"I have a place to go," I said.

"Yeah?"

"My gran's."

"What's your name?"

"Mary Margaret." I gave him the name Gran started calling me after my mom left, when Gran decided my own name wasn't holy enough or whatever. I didn't want him knowing my real name. I was careful about sharing it. I parceled it out sparingly, only to a few of the kids I'd gotten to know on the street. He tilted his head sideways slightly, like he was waiting for more.

"Well, Mary Margaret," he commented after I didn't say anything, "for the last two nights you haven't been at your gran's."

I froze with the little, white plastic spoon halfway to my mouth. How did he know? It meant he'd been watching me for two nights at least. I glanced sideways. There was no one between us and the door. I could make a run for it. And after that I'd have to be more careful, keep my eyes open for anyone watching me.

"Relax," he said, leaning back in his chair, spreading his hands wide. "I'm not telling anyone. No questions. Now eat up." He lifted his chin to indicate the soup in front of me. "If Pheebes was in trouble I'd hope someone would help her out, that's all."

I finished the soup, both rolls, and the coffee.

"Want some more?" he asked. "Dessert?" he suggested.

I shook my head. I was starting to feel full and warm for the first time in days. I was feeling dozy, too, the way you do after a big meal.

"Want a drive to your gran's?" he asked.

"No." I said it louder than I meant to.

His eyes lingered on me for a beat. He shrugged. "That's cool." He checked his watch and stood up. "Listen, I have to go. You take care of yourself. Oh, and here—" He picked up a napkin he'd brought to the table along with the food and scribbled on it. "My phone number. Just in case." He put it on the table in front of me. "If you're in trouble, give me a call. Anytime. Like I say, if Pheebes was in trouble..." And then he left, moving quickly and easily between the chairs and tables and out the door. When I picked up the napkin, two twenty-dollar bills fell out. I checked to see if anyone had noticed, but no one was paying attention. I grabbed them and stuffed them in my jeans pocket.

He'd left his coffee. The cup looked full and I couldn't remember him drinking out of it. I pulled it over and sat with my hands cupped around its heat, sipping from it now and then, trying to make my stay in this warm, well-lit place last as long as possible. Thinking about what had happened with him.

I was trying to figure out what I thought about him. He wasn't like the guys who sidled up to me on the street. You could smell the meanness on those guys. I didn't pick that up from him. He seemed kind; he'd bought me dinner. He hadn't pushed when he figured I was lying. He'd grinned like it was a joke between the two of us. He'd left me the money. But I also felt like I wasn't getting the full story from him, like there was more to him being kind to me than me reminding him of his daughter. If he had a daughter—maybe that was a story he'd made up.

Then one of the Timmie's staff came along swabbing down the tables, picking up garbage, and giving me a look that said, *time for you to go.*

After that I kept a look-out to see if I could catch a glimpse of him hanging around, but I didn't see him.

For as long as the forty dollars lasted, I was able to eat every day. The ache of hunger was gone for a while.

It kept getting colder. I was learning my way around; I'd found a few community kitchens where I could get a meal or two a day, and places I could crash at night. There were people who'd rent a room in a boarding house, and then for a couple of bucks they'd let you stay there overnight on a couch, if there was one. Or if you had a sleeping bag you could roll it out on the floor, and if the couch was taken and you didn't have a sleeping bag you could just crash on the floor. Sleeping on the floor was hard, still, it was warmer than being outside. But you had to be quiet and get out first thing in the morning.

They were pretty sketchy places—I had to sleep with all my clothes on and use my knapsack as a pillow so nothing would get stolen. People might wander in in the middle of the night, maybe high, and sometimes there was a fight and you were all kicked out. Plus the smell, and you ran the risk of picking up bedbugs or some other unwelcome passengers. But I was warm at night.

I took a shot at panhandling. I didn't do it right away because at first, I wanted to be as invisible as possible, I didn't want to put myself out there, but eventually I needed the money. I'd find a corner, sit down, and set a paper coffee cup on the sidewalk in front of me, but people—mostly men—could be creepy. They'd slow down when they got close to me, even older guys in snappy business suits, and their eyes would slide over me measuringly. Some of them dropped coins in the cup, but more of them than I'd have thought at first would smirk at me, or say something they thought was funny but wasn't, like, "What's a nice girl like you doing in a place like this?" A few of them tossed garbage, like cigarette butts or receipts, into the cup. Maybe this amused them? Some of them lectured me on whatever they figured I'd done wrong to end up in this situation, even though they had no idea.

Then there were the slimy ones—men who'd dangle a five-or ten-dollar bill (once a twenty) over the cup and ask, "How badly do you need this, honey?" One guy even licked his lips and winked at me after he said something like this. I stared at him—I felt sick to my stomach. You see someone having a rough time and you hit on them?

Plus sitting on the sidewalk was really cold no matter what I did, no matter how much cardboard I found to tuck under me.

Another problem with panhandling was that I'd find a good location, and then another street person would show up and make it clear this was their territory. One guy picked up my cup with a couple of dollars change in it, dumped the coins into his baseball cap, and threw my cup into the gutter. Then, without even looking at me, he snarled, "Get out of here" in a flat tone, dropped his hat on the sidewalk, and sat down where I'd been. He was way bigger than me and had a death's head inked on his neck, so I cleared out fast. When you're in a situation like that, you learn pretty quickly to choose your battles.

Other times, even if no one made me move along, someone might show up when I'd collected enough to buy a meal and make me hand over the money, pushing me around if I didn't give it to them fast enough. This didn't always happen, but when it did, if they left me any I'd only have enough for a coffee and maybe a donut. A few times one of the other kids I'd gotten to know saw this happen and shared some of their take or bought me a hamburger.

I didn't want to go near the shelters run by social services. The kids I knew on the street said you had to answer a lot of questions, and you could get shunted into foster care if you weren't old enough. I knew my gran would never report me missing. She didn't trust government or bureaucrats or any authority but God, so she wouldn't alert anyone. Still, I wanted to stay under the radar, so I looked for off-grid places to sleep. Plus, the other kids told me there were always chicken hawks hanging around the shelters; you'd be leaving in the morning and there were these guys (always guys) hanging around to hit on you or offer you drugs, or whatever they needed to offer you to get you to come with them. Also, the cops might be there looking for any kids who had gone missing recently. If one of my teachers where I'd been going to school reported my absence, the cops might be looking for me, so I did my best to avoid the shelters.

I'd found the public showers, at least, so I was washing again and didn't look as grubby as I had.

I met other kids who were on their own and we were trying to figure out how to rent an apartment together. We needed first and last months' rent. I tried to get a job, went for interviews at a couple of fast-food places, but I didn't have all the ID I needed, and who was going to hire some hungry-looking kid in grimy clothes anyway? Life went on this way for a while. It wasn't easy, but I was learning to find my way. I knew some people. I felt like I was getting my balance.

One day I went way out to the west end for a job interview. I could tell right away I shouldn't have bothered coming—they'd never hire me—and a heavy sadness settled on me. After the interview, I didn't have bus fare, so I started to walk back, heading for one of the places where I knew I could stay if there was space. I didn't go there much because it was in a rough part of town, but it was late and I was tired.

I was walking along the street when suddenly, out of nowhere, some guys come up and surround me, all older and bigger than me. One of them grabbed me, dragged me into an alley, and pinned me against a wall. It was dark, garbage everywhere, and it smelled of piss. I opened my mouth to yell, but the guy who had a hold of my jacket gave me a lazy grin. He shook his head. "Around here?" he waved his hand to indicate the boarded-up storefronts, the empty streets.

I recognized him from when he'd followed me out of the library, calling, "Hi, how you doing? What's your name?" Really loud and fake-cheerful. "Don't be shy. What's your name?" He'd trailed me for a while, but I'd told him to fuck off, picked up the pace, and lost him after a few blocks.

Now he had his face right up close to mine. I could smell beer on his breath, see the stubble on his chin and the tats ringing his neck. Aside from his earrings, he had an eyebrow ring, and a stud through his lower lip.

"We want what you have," he said, jamming his knee between my knees, levering them apart and shoving his leg up hard.

"I don't have anything." My voice sounded thin and wavery. I was starting to feel sick to my stomach.

For a second I considered kicking out, but there was a bunch of guys and only one of me, and I guessed that if I hurt one of them the rest of them would pound on me, and that might be worse than whatever it was they had in mind. I thought of an opossum playing dead and I went all limp and quiet.

Beer Guy shoved his hand into my jacket pocket and pulled

out what I had in there, a few coins and a pack of gum. His knee was working itself back and forth against my crotch. He was smiling, pressing himself hard against me. He was still smiling when he slapped me—once, twice, my head whipping back and forth. "I got something for you," he said, biting his lower lip and grinding his pelvis into me. I was pulling away but he caught my wrists in his hands and jerked them behind my back.

I felt like I was going to throw up, except I hadn't eaten since morning so there was nothing to throw up, only a bitter taste in my throat. Behind him I saw the faces of the other guys, a blur, I couldn't have said how many there were, only that they were staring blankly—one of them checking his cell, running down some list with an occasional *beep, beep, beep.*

Beer Guy was pressing harder. He pulled one of my hands out from behind my back and was moving it toward his fly. I tried to pull away, then his knee came up again and caught me hard in the crotch. I doubled forward; pain knocked the breath out of me. "Cut the bullshit," he said in a flat tone. His voice never changed. He sounded like he was talking about the weather.

He had his hand clamped on my wrist and was pushing it closer to his fly when an expression of confusion crossed his face, and suddenly he was hanging in front of me, his feet dangling a couple of inches off the ground.

The next moment he flew through the air and smashed into a metal garbage can. He barked in pain before sliding to the ground. The other guys were gone, hightailing it out of there.

Frozen against the wall, I watched Francis walk over to Beer Guy and drag him upright by the hood of his hoodie. Beer Guy gagged and coughed, clutching at his throat.

For a second Francis looked at him, head cocked to one side, as if the guy was a puzzle he was trying to figure out. "Stay away from her," he said to Beer Guy in a low growl. His free hand was balled up in a tight fist.

"What're you going to do, call the cops?" the guy said in a strangled voice that had a sneering tone. "Didn't work too well last time, did it?" Francis dropped him on the ground and turned to me. His mouth was a hard, tight line.

"Come on," he said, putting his arm around my shoulder and hustling me along. "Let's get out of here and get you cleaned up."

On the sidewalk near the alley, I saw some of the coins and the gum Beer Guy had grabbed out of my pockets. I bent down to pick them up and Beer Guy came running out of the alley towards Francis. At the last minute, Francis crouched down, Beer Guy went sailing over him and ended up sprawled on the sidewalk.

He was getting to his feet when Francis kicked out, catching him on the side of his head. The guy went down in a heap. Francis bent over him.

"Unfortunately, he'll probably be fine," he said. "Although he'll have a mother of a headache." He gazed at the crumpled figure. "Asshole," he said in a cold voice. Then he came over to me and led me to his truck. He opened the passenger door, but I stood where I was.

He gave me a level look. "I get it," he said, nodding. "You're scared. But do you really want to stick around here?"

Night had fallen. The street was deserted. It was mostly empty storefronts with plywood-covered windows. There was a coin laundry, a 7-11, and a cheque-cashing place with neon lights flashing in the window. The place I was headed was a couple of kilometers away. I shook my head. If I started talking, I knew I'd end up crying.

"Climb on in, Mary Margaret." He remembered my name, which was on the one hand reassuring, and on the other hand vaguely disturbing. "I'm only doing what I'd do for Pheebes," he said. "Or what I hope someone would do for her. Okay? Get in the truck before those other assholes show up with reinforcements."

I climbed in.

~

That was the beginning. I didn't start travelling with him right away—that came in a couple of weeks. I didn't even know about the trailer then.

He dropped me off at a different place than the one I'd been headed to, a better place he knew about—cleaner, safer, closer to downtown—but not before convincing me to let him buy me some warm clothes the next day, a coat and some new boots.

The situation felt off-kilter, but he seemed to be straight with me. There wasn't any sexy behaviour, no flirting, nothing suggestive. Sometimes he became kind of strict with me, the way I figure a dad might have, if I was being too what he called *sassy*, if I used a word or phrase close to being what I came to understand he thought was off-colour—"You mind your tongue, Miss," he'd say somewhat sharply, with none of his usual kidding around.

Over time I started to think he really did have a daughter about my age, which was why he was looking out for me. I wondered where she was.

And he was always careful to keep space between us. There was the toolbox that sat on the seat beside him, and pretty soon he'd built that wall of fast-food bags, his books, my books, and other odds and ends. When we ate in fast-food places—which we did a lot of the time—he always sat across from me, not beside me.

By the time I saw the trailer a few nights after the Beer Guy incident, he'd heard about my parents, how my dad had bailed on me and my mom when I was two. There were only a few details I remembered about my dad; once in a while I'd get a whiff of beer and cigarettes at the same time and he'd pop into my head, and there were a couple of other, cloudy memories.

I told Francis about some of what had happened, but not all—only enough for him to understand. After my dad left, my mom moved back in with her mom, my gran. I think Mom thought she could tough it out—live with Gran long enough to get on her feet, get a job, find a place for the two of us to live—but Gran, Gran just went after her all the time. About how she'd told Mom my dad was evil, how she'd warned Mom not to get involved with him, but had Mom listened to her? No, she hadn't—and look at how it had all turned out, and now Mom was back home again, with a kid, and if only she'd listened. It went on like that for a long time, and then one morning Mom was gone.

And all I had left of her was a photo Gran threw in the trash one day after Mom left, similar to the one Francis had of Phoebe, but bigger. I grabbed it out of the garbage and hid it. In the photo Mom was sitting on the ground holding fat little toddler me and smiling up at the camera. She was facing into the sun, and her eyes were scrunched up into crescents. There must have been a breeze, because a strand of her hair trailed across her forehead. She looked happy. I thought maybe I remembered the day the picture had been taken; I had a vague memory of a sunny day we'd spent in the park when Dad was still around. I remembered laughter, and Dad giving me a piggyback. But then I thought maybe I didn't really remember the day—maybe what I thought I remembered was what I wanted to have happened.

I had a card from her, too, for a while, one she'd made for my third birthday. She'd folded a plain piece of white paper in half and then folded it over in half again and drawn a heart in red crayon on the front. Inside, the card said, "Happy birthday, muffin! Love, mom." After she left, I kept it tucked away under my mattress, but I must have left it out by accident once and I guess Gran found it, and I never saw it again. So, I'd hidden the photo from Gran really well, and now I carried it around in my knapsack, in one of the secret pockets because if I carried it in my jacket pocket it would get all bent.

I didn't tell Francis about the photo, but I did tell him about missing my mom. But also that I'd seen how sad Gran made my mom, so I understood why she had to leave and I knew it would have been harder for her if she had taken me with her. Just one more thing to keep track of.

What I didn't tell him was that for a long time, I'd hoped she was looking for a place where we could both live, and when she found one, she'd come back to get me. After a while, when she didn't come back, I used to think about trying to find her. I knew my gran wouldn't go looking for Mom. I knew I was too young to leave Gran's to do it on my own. So, I figured I'd have to wait until I was older and then I'd do it. And when I was sad or feeling lonely or missing her, I'd imagine what it would be like to find her, to figure out where she lived and knock on her door. I thought of her opening the door and seeing me there, and how she'd say my name in surprise, and pull me into a hug. And I remembered how she smelled, of soap and some flowery perfume, and how safe and warm it felt when we hugged, and I would burrow into that thought, the thought of us being a family again.

I didn't tell him how after a couple of years when my mom didn't show up, thinking about her got all mixed up with me feeling angry she'd left and hadn't come back to get me. Thinking about her hurt. That was when I decided I could do fine without a family—I'd be better on my own, it would be simpler. Caring about people meant you missed them, or they could hurt you. Not caring was easier.

He'd heard about my crazy gran: her steel grey hair gathered in a tight bun; how she bought only one type of dress—long, way past her knees, made of dark brown cotton with a buttoned-up collar—and she wore the same outfit every day, that dress and a brown cardigan, and her sensible ugly black shoes. I told him some of the less crazy stories about her, like how she bought dented cans of food that had lost their labels because she could get them really cheap. She did this even though she wasn't poor—Mom had told me she wasn't. I can't remember if she was always this way, or if she grew worse after Mom left.

I'd sit at the kitchen table holding the tins up to my ear and shaking them, waiting for her to open them. I'd be trying to figure out what was inside. *Peaches, peaches, please be peaches,* I'd be thinking, but most of the time there'd be soggy, squishy peas inside, or hearts of palm—who decided hearts of palm was food? And we'd have these weird meals—Spaghetti-Os, mixed veg, and cocktail sausages, if we were lucky.

Gran wouldn't have a TV in the house, or a radio. She said they were instruments of the devil. She barely tolerated the old black rotary dial phone in the front room but decided to have it "in case of emergency." No cell phone for her or me.

She'd grab me by my wrist and drag me down on my knees beside her to talk to the Big Guy up in the sky (because she was sure it *was* a guy) if she thought I'd done anything the least bit sinful, like talk back, or say something she thought wasn't the absolute truth. And she talked about the Devil as if she had a straight line to him, too—a direct line to him, and one to the Big Guy. She told me what the Devil would do if I didn't behave—which meant if I didn't do exactly what she wanted me to do, fast—and then I'd have nightmares for a week or more, dreams of swimming in a lake of fire and of listening to the screams of the damned, of which she was sure I was one.

Gran saw the Devil everywhere. Once, we were walking down the street and she saw a woman up ahead of us with her fingernails painted bright, shiny red. I pointed her out and said I thought her nails looked pretty. Gran grabbed my arm and dragged me to the other side of the street. "Stay away from her and anyone with red nails like hers—they work for the Devil."

There was the time she spanked me with a hairbrush when she thought I'd been disrespectful. It was before I started school, so maybe I was three or four. She took me into the bathroom, sat on the toilet, laid me across her knees, and hit my bottom with the hairbrush one, two, three times. It's funny what I remember, not the feeling of the brush hitting me, but the sharp slapping sound of it landing on me, and what I saw out the bathroom window; the back yard with a tall tree by the back fence, the grass a washed-out grey colour under it. I don't remember the spanking hurting, but I do remember the back yard, and the dark green leaves on the tree—more like ragged shadows than leaves—how they fluttered a little in the wind, like they were waving at me.

She made me wear what she called "modest" clothing—nothing tight or bright or colourful, and for sure no short skirts and camisole tops like some of the other girls at school wore. I opted for jeans, dark t-shirts, and runners. She fought me even on those; she believed young women should wear dresses, not pants—long dresses or skirts to my ankles, but I refused. I didn't want to look like a refugee from pioneer times. At school, I still ended up on the wrong side of the invisible line separating the cool kids from everyone else.

So, she was my family. But she didn't feel like family, we didn't feel like a family the way I remembered family feeling when it was Mom and me. Gran and me, what we had was different; what it was, I didn't have a name for.

Francis listened and didn't comment. It was the first time I could remember talking about it with anyone. Who would I have spoken to about it? If I'd mentioned all this at school, I figured they'd call the Children's Aid Society and that would be the end of me living with Gran, which, even though living with her could be hard, was what I knew and I could manage it. Keeping it to myself was easier than telling anyone, but also, it was a secret I had to guard and be careful about. Telling Francis was good, and also strange at the same time. Strange because the weight of it being a secret was gone, good because I felt better, lighter, as if I'd been a bit frozen and now I was thawing.

Telling him put it out there, where I could look at it and see I wasn't crazy for wanting things to be different, and it probably wasn't surprising for all of it to make me sad. And talking to him about it, having him listen and not start telling me what I should do, or saying he was going to take care of it, felt like he understood, which put both of us on the same side of Gran's craziness. I wondered if he might be someone I could trust, but then I thought it's safest to keep yourself to yourself, as Gran used to say, so I parceled out what I told him, gave him the briefest outline.

He didn't push, and I didn't tell him all of it. How my gran knew the End Times were coming, and it was worse to spare the rod than spoil the child. That she really did say, "This hurts me more than it hurts you" when she hit me, which she did if she found out I'd told a white lie or read a book she thought was sinful, which was most books that weren't the Bible. I think she believed it.

It was when she started talking about taking me out of school, because school harboured so much wickedness, that I ran away. I couldn't stand the thought of being stuck in the house with her all day. I knew she thought she was doing the right thing, only the right thing meant hitting me, and us living in a freezing house with no TV, and eating odds and ends from cans, and listening to her talk about the punishments waiting for The Damned on Judgment Day—it wasn't going to be pretty. And The Damned included pretty much everybody except her and me, and she wasn't too sure about me.

Francis listened. After a while, he said, "Sounds like your gran has some demons to contend with," which was a thing she might have said herself about someone else, and which she would have understood. But the way he said it, he wasn't making fun of her, he took her seriously, which I appreciated because even though I couldn't live with her, I knew she was trying to do the best she could for me and she feared for my immortal soul, and I didn't hate her.

3.

GRADUALLY I GREW MORE RELAXED with Francis. He didn't tell me a whole lot about himself, mostly he talked about Phoebe. He seemed happy to have someone he could talk about her with—how she loved horses and wanted to be a vet. He said she'd be a great one, she was so smart. I loved how proud he was of her. I thought she was lucky to have that. I had the feeling he'd been divorced or separated from Phoebe's mother, who he never really mentioned.

Then he showed me the trailer and everything in it, large and small. The interior was cool, full of fascinating gizmos, all the available space cleverly made use of. He showed me how he could flick a switch and two bunks would drop down, suspended from the ceiling by chains. Then he tugged on the chains and fiddled with some mechanical stuff and the bunks were tucked away again.

Being in there was like standing in a shop full of wonderful treasures. He put a tiny sculpture of a rabbit in my hand. It was about the size of a big walnut and so detailed I could see the pupils in the rabbit's eyes, the texture of its fur, the pads on its feet. "This is a netsuke," he said.

"A what?"

He took the sculpture back and turned it over in his hands.

"Netsuke," he repeated. He told me they were made in Japan. In the old days, people in Japan dressed in kimonos, which were like bathrobes except that was their everyday clothing. The kimonos had no pockets, so people had sagemono, small containers that hung from their belts by cords, to carry their money and other essentials around in. The netsuke kept the cords connected. "See the tiny holes the cords went through?" He held up the netsuke and pointed.

That was my first lesson. Francis showed me how carefully the netsuke maker had carved it, the funny precise details he'd put in, how the rabbit's nose was wrinkled like it had caught the scent of something.

He didn't tell me at first what he did. He said he was in the antique business, but he didn't tell me how he acquired the antiques or what he did with them.

One day, about a week and a half after showing me the trailer—I'd found a place to crash at more permanently by then, a house one of brothers of a kid I'd met on the street was house-sitting for six months but he wanted us out of there during the day, I think because he was selling drugs—Francis took me out for breakfast. It was late fall heading into winter and getting harder on the street. The night before it had snowed, a wet, heavy snow that was turning into slush as the day warmed up. Francis said he was going on a business trip, and did I want to come along? "Nothing funny. Just, you might find it interesting."

"What's the catch?" I asked.

He looked surprised and little hurt. "No catch. Why do you assume there's a catch?"

I looked at him. I had learned a lot in the past few months. "Where will we stay?"

"The bunks in the trailer." He seemed pretty pleased with himself. I wasn't sure I liked the set-up.

"It's cold to be sleeping in the trailer," I pointed out.

"Truckers sleep in their trucks all the time," he said, like he was stating the obvious, but then he cocked his head to one side and looked at me as if he suddenly understood. "Here's a better idea: I'll sleep in the truck—I'm cool with that—and we'll get you a room in a motel or a bed and breakfast, warm and cosy."

"I don't know."

"Think about it," he said. "I'll be leaving at the end of the week."

So, I thought about it all day as I trekked from one warm place to the next. As I slogged from a cafe to the library, to another coffee shop, and back to the library, my boots—the ones Francis had bought me and were way better than the running shoes I'd been wearing when we met—were soaked by slush and my feet were cold and damp. My feet were permanently cold and damp in those days. I was always trying to get warm and dry. Sometimes when I was cold and then managed to warm up, my fingers ended up sore and swollen. I was bored with all the walking around. I hadn't been able to find a job, and I was always uncomfortable. I couldn't see circumstances changing soon. If I took Francis up on his offer it would at least be a change. Who knew—maybe I might even learn interesting stuff, see some sights. What he'd told me about kimonos and sagemonos and netsuke had been cool. I'd been curious, so I'd asked one of the librarians to help me find a book about netsuke. She'd looked surprised, but she went into the stacks and tracked down a book about Japanese art and culture, and I read parts of it. I wondered where Francis had learned all this.

I thought I might go with him. I phoned him and we met at a coffee shop.

"That'd be great," he told me, sounding glad. "There's a quality you have—you know how to comport yourself, how to behave. Your gran must have taught you some manners. And when you open your mouth, it isn't a bunch of nonsense that comes out; you speak in complete sentences, you have a wide vocabulary. All that reading of the Bible you must have done. It'll be useful; it'll confer a sheen of respectability on our operation." He broke a muffin into two pieces and pushed the larger part of it across the table to me. "Plus, I forgot to tell you," he said offhandedly, as if he had only this instant remembered. "I'll be able to pay you some."

"For what?"

"Oh, odd jobs," he said, concentrating on sweeping muffin crumbs off the table. "Don't worry—it's all on the up and up. Look at it this way, you'll be picking up some skills."

I nibbled the muffin. "Doing what?"

"I'll show you. There are times when I need some assistance. Nothing you can't handle. Plus, three squares a day."

I figured it couldn't be more boring than what I was doing, and it might even be fun, or at least informative. And if it didn't work out, I could always bail. "Okay," I said.

"Glad to hear it." He held out his hand. We shook on it. He seemed genuinely pleased. "Happy to have you along. I'll pick you up here Friday at eight. Bring your clothes and whatever else you have."

That was when he told me my name was going to be Frances Person, a.k.a. Frankie from then on.

~

He fitted me out with a couple of pairs of new jeans, runners, t-shirts, some sweatshirts, a hoodie with deep pockets. I looked like a million other kids, which I guess was the point.

We started driving back roads, knocking on doors. I watched him and learned how he eased his way first into a conversation with someone, and then into their house or barn.

It went on that way for a while, us picking up baubles and knickknacks for cheap. I guessed Gran would have disapproved of what we were doing, but as far as I could see, no one was really hurt. Those folks made some money and offloaded odds and ends they had no use for, and we acquired inventory and the chance to earn some income.

I grew less guarded with him, accustomed to what we were doing. I even began to trust him, up to a point, or at least I stopped wondering all the time if what he said and what he meant were two different things. He talked about Phoebe a lot, about what the life of a vet would be like, wondering whether she'd enjoy it.

And then, one day, things changed.

4.

IT WAS AN ICY COLD DAY. The night before we'd had the first really heavy snowfall of the season, and now it was overcast and starting to feel like it truly was winter.

We were passing through a dinky place—really only an intersection with a few houses, a post office, a church, a diner, and a garage. Francis pulls over for gas at the garage. I get out and go to the washroom and when I come back, he's chatting with the mechanic, asking him about the fan belt. I'm not sure why—the fan belt snapped last week when we were out in the back of the beyond and Francis fixed it himself, "jerry-rigged," he called it. When we hit the next town, he had it replaced, so why he's asking this guy about it doesn't make sense. But he's talking in a casual tone, the same one he adopts when he has his eye on a potential target, all relaxed and friendly, waiting to see if the person on the other end will pick up the conversational gambit—some don't, most do—and when I show up, he says, "Oh, hey, Guy, this is my daughter Loretta."

"Hi, Loretta," Guy says. He's a tall fellow with a flat, round face, a loose, shambling body with a bit of a tummy sticking out, ragged brown hair poking up in wisps, and a quiet, shy smile. He's wearing blue overalls stained with grease and has a wrench in one hand.

"Hi," I say. Then I step back, out of his line of vision, and lean against the truck.

"About the fan belt?" Francis prompts.

Guy gives his two cents' worth, they jaw back and forth for a while, then Francis asks, "Can you recommend a place me and my daughter can stay? Motel? Cheap and cheerful is what I'm looking for—and clean."

Why is he asking? We're out in the boonies in the middle of the week. There's nothing going on around here, no flea markets, no church rummage sales. Why would we make a pit stop here? What's up with that?

Guy reaches up and scratches his head, then remembers he has oil all over his hands and pulls his hand out of his hair. "Nothing around here," he says. "Closest place is the Twin Pines about 10 'k that way." He waves the wrench back the way we just came. "They're pretty good."

Then Francis says, "How long have you lived around here?" I'm trying to understand what's up, but I know better than to interrupt.

"All my life," the fellow says.

"You're lucky," Francis says warmly. "I'd love to live in a place like this. I've had enough of being on the road. Maybe after this trip. Any places for sale around here?" If I hadn't been watching him closely—alerted by his exaggerated enthusiastic manner—I might have missed the look he threw me: *pay attention*.

Guy looks down at the wrench he's holding, frowns like this is a real challenging question. There's a moment's pause. "Yeah, up the road a ways." He points the wrench in the direction we were heading. "Couple of concession lines over. A nice place."

"Oh, yeah?"

"Yeah. Mrs. Hancock. Sweet lady. Her husband died right after Christmas last year and she's on her own now."

Francis shakes his head. "You know, same thing happened with my wife," he says, his voice going low and mumbly. "She made it through the holidays and all—I think she held on for Loretta, and then she just..." He lets the words trail off, implying sorrow, a still-raw wound. He clamps his jaw shut tight, blinks a couple of times.

"Sorry to hear that," Guy says gruffly.

"Yeah." Francis coughs, clears his throat. "You think time will—" he looks up, over Guy's shoulder at the grey sky, lost in thought for a moment. Then he seems to remember himself, shakes his head, dismissing bad memories. "Anyway, that house? A mile up the road, a couple miles? Sorry—a couple 'k? I'm showing my age." He grins. "This seems like a fine place to raise a kid."

"You go up to the next concession road, take a left—" Guy gives Francis directions.

"Any schools nearby?" Francis asks, raising his eyebrows at me.

"Over in the next town. The kids are all bussed."

"What's the place look like?"

"White with blue gingerbread trim," Guy says. "There's an oak tree in the front yard."

"Well, it's mighty tempting. Thank you for all your help," Francis says.

~

Francis says there are three major stages in life: birth—your own and other people's—marriage—your own and other people's—and death—preferably other people's. According to his observations, any of these three stages leads to big changes, and in times of big change, that's when people are most likely to shuck off their belongings, the way a caterpillar moults before it becomes a butterfly. During those times, he says, objects in proximity to the big change lose their specific gravity, they become lighter and have a tendency to grow unmoored and float away. It becomes easier then, to separate the objects from their owners, the people from their things, because people mostly aren't interested in material goods at those times, they're focused on the changes underway.

"We're doing these folks a favour," he tells me. "They're embarking on a new stage of life. Why would they want to carry all their old junk along with them? It's a burden. They need new accoutrements for their new lives. We take away the old flotsam and jetsam and give them the money to buy the new supplies they need. They should be thanking us."

The lady who'd been widowed; we drive along the road Guy told us, maybe three or four kilometers. The town falls away fast, and the highway takes us south, deking and winding through gently hilled land. There are trees on either side of the road: maples, aspen, poplar, spruce. Francis has been teaching me about trees, the difference between hardwoods and softwoods, which ones are best for construction, which for furniture. The forest opens out every once in a while, and we get a glimpse of a field or the shoreline of a lake not too far away.

We see farmhouses, mostly modest, red brick, and close to the road. Now and then there's a larger pile, built by city people who are coming in and gobbling up farmland to construct huge homes they can escape to on the weekend.

We find the place and drive a couple hundred meters past it, pull off onto the shoulder of the road. I unclasp my seatbelt, and I'm about to climb out when Francis puts his hand on my arm. "Hold on," he says softly.

I turn to look at him.

"We're going to play it a little differently this time, Frankie," he says. "Up to this point it's all been above board and out in the open, now the rules are going to change. When we get in there—"

he glances over his shoulder at the widow's house "—because we will get in there, I want you to keep your eyes peeled. I want you to be on the lookout for. . ." He pauses, choosing his words carefully. "Let's call them unassuming, easily transferable items. Nothing big, nothing flashy. Items of value that might not be immediately missed upon our departure. Because I want some of those items to transfer out of the house with you when we leave, if you get my drift." He shifts his gaze to me, his eyes intent.

I go still. It's as if time has slowed down. I feel kind of sick to my stomach. He stares at me and I stare back, frozen, like a mouse being watched by a cat. What can I do? Here I am out on an empty road in the middle of nowhere. No one knows or cares where I am. If I say no, does he drive off and leave me here? Or something worse?

Then he chuckles and jostles my arm gently. "It's a game, Frankie. Grab a couple of tiny items—some inconspicuous gew-gaws she won't miss. It's no big deal. We add to our inventory, she's none the wiser." He shrugs. "Just a game," he says. "No one gets hurt."

He opens the truck door and climbs out. "Come on, let's go."

We cross the road and walk back to the house, glancing around as if we're lost. Francis has a piece of paper in his hands with stuff scribbled on it, so it looks like we're reading directions, even though he didn't write down the directions. He doesn't need to; as I've learned, he can remember precisely what Guy said, word for word. But this way, he tells me, it'll look like we don't really know what we're doing. We'll seem somewhat lost, which guarantees the marks will underestimate us, and that gives us the upper hand.

We approach the house with blue gingerbread trim. As we walk towards it, he tells me you can see it was once neat and shipshape, but that was a while ago. Now, he points out in a low voice as we get closer, the paint on the window frames is peeling, and the shingles on the roof are curling.

We walk up the gravel driveway—only a few steps, really—and follow a path across the lawn, nothing more than footsteps worn into the grass, the indentations dusted with snow, that leads to the front door. Francis knocks. After a minute, a woman opens the door.

She's short, not much taller than me, and I'm not big. She has a puffy, slightly wrinkled face. Her hair is thin and permed into a frizz. It's an odd, tired yellow colour at the ends, like the stain on smokers' fingertips. Her roots are white. She looks about my gran's age, in her seventies, but where my gran is hard and pointy, she's soft and plump, a series of curves squeezed into a pale blue sweatshirt with pink and white flowers painted on it that have mostly been worn off in the washing machine. Her pants are dark blue and shapeless. She has slippers on, and even this early in the day she looks tired.

"Sorry to bother you," Francis says, smiling apologetically.

She doesn't respond. She looks at him in silence. Which means she hasn't slammed the door in his face. Which means we have a chance. It isn't a yes, but it isn't a no, and Francis has taught me there's a lot of room to maneuver in the space between yes and no.

"We heard—my daughter and I—" he scoots sideways so she can see me standing behind him. She glances at me, then back at him. "—there's a house might be on the market hereabouts. Pleasant young fellow back at the garage. My wife, well—" again the words breaking up like a radio going to static, again his voice fading. When he says this, the woman's eyebrows rise slightly, and she focuses on him more intently. Francis straightens his shoulders, clears his throat. "Anyway, we need a change. My name is Joe, by the way. Joe Williams."

She nods.

"And we heard—"

She turns around and starts shuffling to the back of the house, her slippers dragging on the ground as if it's too much work for her to lift her feet all the way up for each step. She rolls to one side slightly when she walks—a bad hip, maybe, like my gran.

Francis looks at me, I look back. She hasn't invited us in, but she hasn't shut the door, either. He turns away, his gaze locks on her retreating figure, and, with a small hop, skips over the threshold and saunters along behind her. I follow him, shutting the door behind me.

Inside, it's shadowy. The floor in the hallway is wide planks, probably original to the house—like I say, spend enough time with Francis and you learn these things. The place has a musty smell, a mix of old cigarette smoke, a lemony cleaner, and old-house damp.

We follow her down a hall into a roomy kitchen with a table in the middle—a yellow Formica-topped number with chrome ridges all around the sides—and on the other side of it, a window looking into the back yard. The linoleum on the floor is worn and uneven. The cabinets are harvest gold. "Probably last painted in the 1970s," Francis whispers to me while she's taking a cup and saucer, a spoon, and a cereal bowl off the table and setting them in the sink. The fridge and stove are the same colour as the cupboards. Through the window I see a lawn covered with snow and surrounded by tall trees.

On the table are old plastic placemats with autumn leaves trapped inside, the same way in kindergarten we ironed leaves between two sheets of wax paper. There are black and white dog and cat ceramic salt and pepper shakers sitting on a bright red napkin in the middle of the table. The dog perches on its haunches, begging. It has holes poked into its head, spelling out "S." The cat is rolling on its back. The holes poked in its stomach spell "P." There's also a wire serviette dispenser, and a sugar bowl with a lid. Knick-knacks, Francis calls items like these, tchotchkes, dust collectors. A dime a dozen, he says. They're not what we're after.

"I'm thinking of selling," she says. Her voice is somewhat wobbly and breathy, as old people's voices can be. The way she talks, she moves her mouth as little as possible, swallowing parts of the words. *I'm thinkin uv sellin.* "Coffee?" she asks.

"Only if you're having some, thanks," he says.

She spoons some ground coffee out of a red tin into a coffeemaker.

"And why's that, if I may ask?" he says.

"My husband passed." The words are plain, but you can sense the sadness behind them.

"I'm sorry to hear it," Francis says after a short silence.

Her lips tighten; her chin crimps. "Too much room for me now." She's pouring water into the coffeemaker. She waves her free hand to indicate the high-ceilinged kitchen, the entire house.

"How many bedrooms?"

"I'll show you around." *I'll show y'roun.*

We wait for the coffee to brew. No friendly chat, no "patter," as he calls it, in these situations. No salesmanship. He says it would land wrong. "That's for markets, garage sales, the like—where people expect it."

"Now, what would the little girl like?" she asks, and smiles at me. She has a warm smile. "Glass of milk? I have some cookies I keep around for my grandchildren." She turns away to rummage through one of the cupboards. "Not that they visit nearly often enough." She pulls out a yellow box, rips open a plastic wrapper and puts four oatmeal cookies on a plate she carries over to the table, along with the glass of milk.

By now the coffee is ready. She pours out a mug for him and a mug for herself. They add milk and sugar, and she leads him out of the kitchen. I hear the stairs creak as the two of them go upstairs, hear their muffled footsteps overhead as they walk in and out of rooms, hear the murmur of their voices. I pour the milk down the sink, break up one of the cookies, and wash the crumbs down the drain. I don't have the heart to let her know how much I hate that kind of cookie.

While they move around upstairs, I go through the kitchen drawers to see if there are any items of value, but everything in them is old and worn and depressing. I sit at the kitchen table and stare at the back yard. There's an impressive maple tree at the far end, with a swing made from a big truck tire hanging down from one of the thick branches. I think about her grandchildren playing on the swing on hot summer days, or climbing the tree, how it would smell of grass, and the shade under the tree would be cool in the heat of the day.

After a while I hear them come back downstairs. "What a lovely little table, Jean." I catch Francis's voice as they circle through the front parlour on their way back to the kitchen.

"My great-grandmother's," she says. She comes into the room and sits beside me at the table, plucking a cookie from the plate. "She brought it over from Sweden."

He stands in the kitchen door, taking in the room. "It'll be a big move," he observes.

"I'm not looking forward to it," she says, shaking her head. "My sons'll help me, but..."

"I know what you mean," he says. He comes into the room and stands by the table, reaching down for a cookie. "When her mother died—" he swings his coffee cup in my direction "—I put it all in storage. Couldn't stand to go through it. Couldn't stand the memories."

"Yup," she says.

"You should see the table," he says to me, his eyes sharp. "In the front parlour. Quality work there." He turns to the old lady. "If that's all right," he adds.

"That's fine," says Jean, smiling at me.

So, I wander into the parlour. Yes, indeed, it is an elegant little wooden table, standing on delicate tapered legs, hand-carved, with a motif of acanthus leaves around the edge.

Shelves run across one whole side of the room crammed with what Frances calls bibelots: glass paperweights, ceramic figures of old-fashioned milkmaids and shepherds flirting with each other, paper-thin porcelain teacups sitting on paper-thin porcelain saucers, each set decorated with a different flower: violets, forget-me-nots, sweet Williams, roses. Dozens and dozens of things.

"It's pretty," I say, walking back into the kitchen.

They're sitting at the table. Francis has finished his first cookie and has the last of the four in his hand.

I sit down and they chat for a while longer, Francis mostly asking questions and listening to her answers, making sympathetic noises. It goes on like this for fifteen, twenty minutes. After a while—after we hear about her dead husband, a welder, and her two boys, who've moved to big cities and don't visit frequently enough. About her arthritis and how the storm windows have to be put up each winter and taken down each spring, and what with her friends and neighbours moving away or passing, it's getting harder and harder to find someone to do it, no matter how much she pays, and goodness, she sure can't be going up and down a ladder with those windows—after it's gone on like this for a while, Francis winds it up.

"I know what you mean," he says. "It's hard, all right." Then he stands up. "Thank you. It's a beautiful house. Let me give you my phone number." He pulls a pen out of his jacket pocket, scratches a number on the corner of the sheet of paper he's been carrying. He tears off the number and gives it to her. She takes it, gives it a quick look, then tucks it in one of her pants pockets. She stands up and we all walk down the hallway to the front door.

On the doorstep he turns. "I'm sorry for your loss, Jean." His hand rests lightly on her shoulder for an instant. "Keep me in mind if you decide to sell, okay?"

She nods. "Glad to meet you," she says. "And your daughter, too." She smiles at me, and right then I hate him.

~

We walk back to the truck and drive away. When we're well out of sight of the house, he pulls over onto the shoulder of the road. "So, what'd you get?"

I pull a paperweight out of one of the hoodie pockets—a beautiful piece, heavy, solid, with a millefiori centre. I set it in his hand. He turns it over, squints at the name etched on the bottom. I took it off one of the high shelves. I brushed away the dust that had settled around it where it had been sitting so there wouldn't be a clear, undusted circle to give away its absence. I also shifted a tiny porcelain bird next to it sideways a couple of centimeters, to fill in the space left behind.

He purses his lips and sets it on top of the toolbox on the seat between us. "Not bad," he says. "I bet she didn't even know what she had. Probably picked it up for cheap at a yard sale or a flea market. What else?"

I hand him a miniature figure I found at the back of one of the lower shelves, a rounded shape carved out of bone, fluid lines flowing together to form a polar bear walking. I like how it sits in my hand, how smooth the curves feel when I run my thumb over them, and the feeling I get when I do that, quiet, still.

He scrutinizes it, turns it over, frowns, grimaces in irritation. "Worthless," he says. "Here." Passing it back to me. "Don't say I never gave you anything." I roll the bear over, hold it up to examine it more closely. It has a tiny, elegant snout and two tiny holes drilled in for eyes. I slip it back into my pocket.

"What else?" he demands. I finger a pin in my pocket, tucked behind the bone sculpture, nearly weightless, elegant, slender, with a row of pearls set along it. I shake my head. He looks over at me. His chin sinks, an eyebrow rises. His mouth curves slightly. Then, before I know what's happening, his arm shoots out and the palm of his hand catches my cheek. It's a smooth, efficient movement. My head jerks sideways, my eyes water. Gran's hit me harder, but coming out of the blue like this, it surprises me, which makes it scary. I pull away from him, huddle against the door.

"Give it." He grips the steering wheel with his left hand and holds out his right, not even looking at me now, his eyes on the road ahead of us. I set the pin on his palm. "You ought to know by now, Frankie," he says lightly. "Never try to con a con."

He holds the pin up close to his face, eyes the pearls, turns it over, looking for a maker's mark. "Excellent," he says. "You have a good eye." He slips it into his shirt pocket and taps it lightly with one hand, as if he's making sure it's there. "Not a bad day's work," he says. "Still, I wish I'd been able to figure out a way to get that table out of there."

Only three items taken, I think. Not much, considering all she had. She'll notice eventually, maybe soon, maybe not for a while. I imagine her looking at the top shelf one day wondering, frowning. Trying to figure out why it looks different, whether there's something missing, running through a list in her mind. She might even bring a chair in from the kitchen—she'd never stand on the little table the way I did. She'll climb up cautiously, her balance uncertain, peer around, wonder if she's losing her memory. It'll be months before she notices the bear is missing, if ever. The pin, I wasn't too sure about. But will she connect the disappearances with the pleasant man, the widower, who dropped in one morning, and his daughter, a quiet girl? What was his name again? She'll ask herself, standing up there, peering at the shelf. Didn't he write it down for her? She'll climb down, carry the chair back to the kitchen, shuffle through the pile of letters, bills, and flyers on the corner of the counter. Frown again, trying to remember.

If she finds the paper and tries the phone number, she'll learn it never existed. No point in trying to track down Joe Williams, either, if she remembers the name he gave. There's thousands of Joe Williamses out there.

"Anyway, we've lightened her load a mite when it comes time for her to move."

I sit and stare straight ahead. I don't say anything, but the connection between us is fractured, and from now on a part of me will always be watching him.

5.

FRANCIS SAID THERE WERE A FEW more things he had to *elucidate*, that we were getting to the end of what he called my *initiation process*.

I thought about what had happened. After the surprise wore off, I looked at the situation. I'd stolen three items from Jean. Nothing big. Nothing really valuable. There'd been an etched crystal glass with a gold rim I'd left, and a tiny, delicate silver bowl I could have lifted but didn't. I knew Gran would say stealing is stealing, and I'd burn in hell for doing it—it would be that simple for her. That was one of the good things about my gran: she wasn't complicated. I always knew exactly where I stood with her.

But for me, the situation wasn't so simple. Francis made it seem like a game, like, how much could we get away with? And he pointed out no one was going to starve, or even suffer much, because of what we took. "At the most, it's an inconvenience," he said.

Which was probably true, but it was still stealing. That was part of what he was doing—and I was doing it, too. Stealing.

I had to admit, compared to how I'd been living before, he mostly took good care of me. I had a warm place to sleep, usually there was enough to eat. I was learning, picking up information, and despite what we were doing, most of the time I felt safe. Plus, he always gave me some cash—not a lot, not so much I could take off and leave him, but enough to buy a book sometimes, a chocolate bar. Yes, there had been that slap, but afterwards he went back to being his usual charming self.

I decided I could stay with him at least for a while, and do what he wanted, but only partly. If he wanted me to take things, I would, but not the best pieces, not the most valuable. In a way I'd actually be protecting people by making sure the best items stayed with them.

The next step, he told me, was the antique markets. I wasn't sure what he meant, but he said, "You're a smart cookie, Frankie. Just watch and all will become clear."

Our first time out was to a market inside a sprawling building, maybe in Kitchener, I'm not sure. There are certain details I remember clearly from those first days, before I understood exactly what the game was, but lot of that time is fuzzy, like when you're traveling on road for the first time and it seems to take a long time because you're paying attention to all the particulars, but by the third or fourth trip along the route, it zips past in a blur. It was the same with the markets; the first few I was so focused on paying attention to what he was doing and wanted me to learn, not much else registered.

There was a lot to pick up. I was focusing on specifics, such as keeping my eyes open for security, learning how to watch without being watched, picking up how to pick items up. Plain, obvious facts, like what town we were in, often escaped me. A question of perspective, I guess.

Once I understood the basics, I started to keep track of the places we hit. There didn't appear to be a pattern I could see, but maybe that was the point; if I could see a pattern, someone else could, and Francis didn't want that.

Anyway, the first time out, the market was inside a boxy cinder-block building. "Circa the 1950s, but with the details tarted up to look oldey timey," said Francis. "Sit here." He pointed at a bench near the front door with a clear view of the place. "Keep an eye on me. And if anyone comes along and asks what you're doing, you're waiting for your father."

"Okay."

"Right. Now, watch."

Bit by bit, I clued in to what he was up to. It was like having a door to a new place slowly opened and entering that world a step at a time. I watched him move around the market, saw how he went from stall to stall in what looked like a random way. I watched him pick up objects, examine them as if he was thinking about buying them, and put them back down.

When we left the market, he had me walk back to the trailer at a distance from him. "You're not following me. Make sure no one would ever guess you're following me." Once we were back at the trailer, he showed me what he had lifted and how he'd done it. Then he had me practice doing it myself with items in the trailer. Little objects at first. "Your hands aren't large enough for the big pieces. But you're still growing. Give it time. You're a natural at this." He pointed out the practicality of the hoodie he'd bought me, the deep pockets, perfect for stashing goods in, then he added, "You have great reflexes, smooth." I liked getting a compliment, even though it was for something I had doubts about—stealing.

He educated me on shell games and told me to keep my eyes open. "Never assume you're the only one doing this. There's marks out there who will turn the tables and stiff you, given half a chance." He didn't sound resentful or angry when he said this, just matter-of-fact.

He told me about bait and switch. "The classic bait and switch is a sales trick," he said. "Those ad guys—they're playing the game same as us, only they're wearing expensive suits and haircuts. With your classic bait and switch, you entice a customer into the store by offering for cheap something people really, really want—say, a top-of-the-line vacuum cleaner for a couple hundred bucks. Except, when the mark arrives, 'Oh, so sorry, we're all sold out. However, since you're here, it so happens we have this other only marginally less marvelous item at half the price of the advertised one.' And a lot of the time the customer will settle for the less costly item.

"Bait and switch is where you offer someone something they think they want, but when they try to close the deal, what's on offer is something other than they expected. The old switcheroo. Keep your eyes open for it—eventually someone's going try and pull it on you."

He demonstrated other maneuvers and told me with practice, I'd be able to master them in no time.

"The beauty of you being my assistant is, if you're caught, you're only a kid, so it's no big deal. A slap on the wrist. They'd probably scold me more than you." He pretended to be a cop shaking his finger. "'Mr. Person, you really have to keep a better eye on your daughter.' 'Yes, officer.'" He looked properly ashamed.

Except, of course, if I'd been caught, he wouldn't be hanging around to help me out. But I didn't learn that until later.

~

We hit antique markets, flea markets, church bazaars, yard sales, rummage sales—any place where items might be changing hands.

Christmas was coming. I started to hear Christmas carols and cheesy, upbeat Christmas songs on the car radio and in the gas stations when we stopped to fill up and buy snacks; decorations began appearing; I saw Christmas cards for sale—all the holiday-related paraphernalia Gran scorned. According to her, none of that nonsense was related to the birth of Our Saviour, and if you "followed those practices," as she put it—gave out Christmas cards, sang the pop Christmas songs—you were a heathen and headed straight to Hell.

I noticed the closer Christmas grew, the quieter Francis became. He didn't kid around as much as usual, making jokes and puns. We'd drive in silence, only the radio playing, none of his usual chat. But I was used to Christmas being dull and low-key, so that was pretty much business as usual to me.

Then, one evening as we were eating at a burger place, he says, "It'll be Christmas soon. Time to dump some of our inventory in exchange for some good, hard cash. We can turn a tidy profit this time of year, if I can find the right venue. We're looking for flea markets, church rummage sales, those sorts of opportunities. Keep your eyes peeled for signs."

"How? We're too late to rent a table to sell stuff."

"Rent a table?" He raised his eyebrows at me. "I've never rented a table in my life. No, it's a matter of 'where there's a will, there's a way,' and all that." He wiped his hands on a napkin and stood up to go.

The next day was Friday. We were driving through a town—small, nestled close to a large lake—and I pointed out a poster on a telephone pole advertising a Christmas rummage sale from 9-4, Saturday and Sunday at St. George's on King Street. "Okay," he said. "That's tomorrow sorted."

We drove around until we came to the Lakeshore Inn, a modest family-run place. While we were checking in, Francis said to the woman behind the counter, "About this Christmas sale at St. George's?"

"Yup?" she said, continuing to type our information into the computer.

"Is it worth a visit while we're here?"

"Well, *I* think so," she replied, squinting at the screen, then deleting some stuff. "But that's because my sister's there, and my cousin."

"What do they sell?"

She looked at him over the top of the monitor. "My sister's a crochet wizard. She can crochet anything—baby clothes, afghans, mitts, hats, sweaters—you name it."

"Sounds impressive."

"And my cousin, she's got more of a craft table: decoupage, macrame, handmade cards. She sells some of her friends' work, too."

"Are there any 'antique—'" he made air quotes with his fingers "—you know, vintage tables there, collectibles, tiny treasures? Maybe pick up a little something for—" he angled his shoulders, blocking me from the conversation, talking in a lowered, confidential tone "—someone?"

"For sure," I heard her say, "My sister-in-law, she'll be there. She has collectibles, antique jewelry, vintage clothing. She's beside the snack bar."

"Perfect, thanks."

~

The next day—not right when the rummage sale opened, but about an hour later, when things were starting to get busy and people were beginning to show up—we arrived at the church. I had my knapsack slung over my shoulder. The sale was in the basement where the walls were painted the same pale institutional green colour I'd seen in lots of other church basements and in school gyms. The scents of beeswax candles, shortbread cookies, and potpourris for sale at some of the tables couldn't mask a faint, musty smell.

We made a beeline for the lady's sister-in-law.

While she talked to a clutch of chatty customers, who were clearly friends of hers, Francis made a show of picking up some of the items on her table, examining them, and setting them down. Once the group drifted off, he stepped closer, waved his hand to indicate her display, and said, "You have some attractive pickings here."

She was straightening a set of silver souvenir spoons her friends had toyed with. She looked up and gave him a salesperson's bright, shiny, one-size-fits-all smile. "Glad you like them."

"How long have you been in the business?" He invested the question with a hint of humour. Conversation, not an interview.

"Oh, all my life," she said, tapping the spoons into line. "My mom used to do it, and she taught me everything I know."

"Well, I have my daughter here." He looked quickly in my direction. *Pay attention*, his look said. "We're on our way out west. I lost my wife—" He paused, cleared his throat "—and my daughter and I, we're heading back to my family.

The woman became serious, a concerned expression on her face as she looked from him to me and back. "Sorry for your loss."

"Thanks," he said, ducking his head in sad acknowledgement. "As it happens, I'm pulling a trailer full of stuff, but it's more than I want to drive all the way out there. The price of gas these days! And the truck's a real gas guzzler. I hadn't realized. So, we're looking to lighten our load a little. I have a few items I'd like to unload—just some knickknacks. I thought I'd keep them to remember my wife by, but it turns out remembering isn't the problem—it's impossible to forget her." For a moment he seemed lost in thought. Then he straightened his shoulders. "Can I show you?" If I hadn't known this was all a lie, I would totally have believed his performance.

"Sure, happy to take a look." She sounded eager to help.

Customers drifted up, then wandered away. I stepped closer and slipped the knapsack off my shoulder. "If you can move any of these, I'd be grateful," said Francis.

Slowly, item by item, he brought out articles: a crystal salt and pepper shaker with silver tops, a set of four silver dinner knives with softly gleaming mother-of-pearl handles, four sterling silver mint julep cups. Each time he set a new object on the table, the woman picked it up and examined it. "Small pieces," he'd told me when he was making his selection the night before. "Quality, but nothing big or too pricey. It has to be able to fly off the table."

"These are real nice."

"They're the genuine article, too. Look—" He turned the cup over and showed her the name on the bottom.

"Quality," she said approvingly. "Well," she said in a business-like tone, "I'll see what I can do for you."

Then, last of all, he pulled out a silver sugar bowl, creamer, and sugar spoon set. Each item was delicately shaped, with handles designed to look like graceful, twining vines. The woman picked up the spoon and turned it over in her hands, shaking her head. "This is beautiful."

"If you think you can move them, that'd be great. I'll give you a cut. What say I leave them with you for the day and I'll check back later? If nothing sells, no problem. I'll collect 'em and be on my way."

She took a deep breath. "Okay. Could you write down what you want for each of them—" her hand swept across the items laid out on the table. "I'll give it a try."

"Thank you," he said, all gratitude. "Thanks so much."

As we walked away, he said to me in a low voice, "She's going to buy that creamer and sugar bowl for herself."

When we went back at the end of the day, she had sold almost all the items Francis had left with her—only a set of delicate opera glasses in mother-of-pearl remained. As she was counting out the bills into his hand, she grinned guiltily. "I bought myself an early Christmas present. That sugar bowl and creamer. Just had to have them. I've never seen another set like it, and they're so lovely."

He pocketed the money and winked at her. "You have an excellent eye. It was a sweet set. I wish I could have kept it, but I'm glad it's gone to a good home." He shook her hand. "You take care. And thanks again."

In the truck he told me, "Couple more as lucrative as that, and we're set 'til the new year."

~

We managed to offload more items at other rummage sales, but not as many as he'd hoped.

Christmas Day came and went quietly, and it felt like business as usual to me.

We seemed to travel around aimlessly for a while. During the first couple of weeks in the New Year, Francis slept in the trailer and paid for a room for me. Then it grew really cold and even with the heater blowing full blast, the cab in the truck never warmed up much. At the end of a frigid day, when we were looking around for a place to stay that night he said, "Frankie, I have a favor to ask."

"Yeah?"

"It's mighty cold today."

I agreed it was.

"I don't think I can sleep in the truck tonight. I don't want to run the risk of freezing tender parts of me. And we're on the negative side of the balance sheet, so I can't afford two rooms."

I knew this. The last few stops hadn't produced much inventory or income.

"I'm wondering if you'd be all right with us sharing a room tonight. If it makes you uncomfortable you have to tell me right now." I was quiet for a minute. Could I be okay with it, or would I stay awake all night worrying?

"How about this," he said, "I'll sleep in the bathtub. Shut the door, and tuck myself in. You can put a chair underneath the door handle to keep it shut. I'll show you how." I had to laugh at the idea of him squashed into a bathtub. "No, I'm serious," he said. "You know, if it was Pheebes in this situation..."

So, I said okay, we could try it. I figured if the situation felt weird or unsafe I could make enough noise to bring help.

It went fine. He showed me how to prop a chair under the bathroom door handle to keep the door shut. "And if you have to, ah, use the facilities during the night, knock loudly and give me time to open the door. I'll stand outside." Then he carried the two pillows and the blankets from one of the two beds in the room into the bathroom, shut the door, told me to put the chair in place, and he didn't come out until morning. Even then he called through the closed door, "Are you decent?"

"Yup," I said.

~

"That wasn't too bad," he said, over bacon and eggs at the motel restaurant, rubbing the back of his neck. "A bit of residual stiffness. Better than frostbitten fingers and toes, though."

Another time we checked into a motel as father and daughter, and Francis said, "I'm bagged—going to catch a few z's." And he collapsed on one of the twin beds. I sat up in my bed and watched, waiting for him to wake up and move into the bathroom. After a while he began to snore, rolled onto his side, and pulled the blanket over himself. I stood up, pushed my bed further away from his and moved the bedside tables between the beds like a miniature wall, then climbed back into bed again and fell asleep sitting up. When I woke in the morning, I was still upright, propped against the headboard of the bed, and he was still fast asleep in the clothes he'd worn yesterday. After that I relaxed about our sleeping arrangements.

Then, if we needed to and had the funds, we'd sign into a motel or a bed and breakfast. I liked B&Bs better than motels. At B&Bs we usually had separate rooms next to each other. "My daughter has nightmares," Francis would say. "So, I like to be nearby." But that wasn't the real story.

At the motels we'd share a room with two twin beds. The reason I liked B&Bs better was because in the motels, most of the time I'd go to bed first and he'd pace. In the motels, I often fell asleep watching him walk from one end of the room to the other and back again. Back and forth for hours. He was quiet, but I knew he was there and I knew he was moving. Even when I was asleep, I sensed it, and when we shared a room, people—friends and strangers alike—stalked silently through my dreams, walking to the same rhythm he did. The only time he didn't pace was if we slept on the bunks in the trailer. Which, now I was more comfortable with him, we did once in a while. He didn't pace in the truck—there was no room for it. Maybe he felt safer there.

Plus, in the motels he kept the light on his side of the room turned on. I had to stick my head between two pillows to block out the light.

There were times in the motels when I'd surface from sleep in the middle of the night and he'd be wide awake, sitting in a chair. Sometimes he'd be staring at me, which freaked me out the first few times it happened. But then I realized he wasn't staring at *me*, he was simply staring, zoned out—gazing straight ahead at the wall, as often as not, or at whatever was out the window.

The best set-up we ever had was on the outskirts of St. Catharines, some chain hotel at the edge of the town. Turned out we were given a suite—two rooms, in fact—because they were out of regular rooms. I took the bedroom and he stretched out on the couch in the other room with the TV turned on low. When I woke up in the morning, it was quiet. I climbed out of bed and cracked the door between the rooms open as quietly as I could. He was out cold on the couch, and there was a program on the TV, a bunch of women sitting around a table shouting at each other, but the sound was turned down and I couldn't tell what they were talking about.

~

The days started getting longer. As the weather warmed up, the sky was changing from flat, icy blue to a deeper, darker tone. Winter was moving towards early spring out there on those roads that always seemed empty and deserted when Francis changed, his state of mind shifted. He seemed to grow clearer, sharper, like the image in a camera coming into focus. Relaxed, easy going Francis disappeared and it seemed like he turned into a different person. His eyes appeared to grow paler, his sentences shorter. There was an edge to him. The twinkle in his eye was gone, instead there was a glint. He was less kicked-back, seemed to get angry more easily. When someone cut him off in traffic he'd yell. "Asshole! Idiot! Your head's so far up your ass you can't see where you're going." I was glad the truck window was rolled up tight. I thought about the slap and wondered if that was the way his mood was going. If it was, I didn't plan to stick around.

One night, we checked into a motel. We ordered takeout,

and he let me pick. I chose Chinese. It was fun, almost like a celebration. After dinner he went into the bathroom and took a long shower. When he came out, he was wearing clothes I hadn't seen before—new and clean—and toweling his hair dry.

"I'm going out," he said. "Call the front desk if you need anything, but don't let anyone in unless you know it's someone from the motel or me. I'll be back late."

The door shut behind him with a click. This was the first time he'd left me alone at night, and it felt peculiar to be an unfamiliar place all on my own. I turned on the TV. When TV grew boring, I turned it off and went to sleep.

A scratching noise woke me up, like the sound of a huge rat clawing away at something. At first, I thought I was having a nightmare. I sat up and looked at the clock radio on the bedside table; it read 3:17, which seemed like a real time, not the kind of time you'd have in a dream.

By now I was wide awake, and I'd figured out the scratching was coming from the hallway door. Someone was trying to get into the room. There was a window high up in the wall beside my bed. If I was going to get out of the room, I'd have to drag a chair over and climb out that way, but all I had on was the white, short-sleeved t-shirt and baggy grey sweatpants I slept in. Where were my shoes?

Right then the door swung open, and there stood Francis, a dark shape against the bright light in the hallway. He swayed slightly and looked around as if he was getting his bearings. I could feel my heart thudding in my chest. I was relieved it was him, but also worried—he didn't seem normal. When the light flooding into the room fell on me, he froze. His eyes locked on me, and in an instant, he'd jumped over the beds between us and grabbed my shoulders. His breath smelled smoky and sour. Automatically I ducked and put up my arm, shielding my face the way I had when Gran lost it, even though it didn't feel like he was going to hit me. It felt like he was excited to see someone I wasn't.

He stopped. "Phoebe?" His voice was faint, puzzled. He frowned, and even though he was staring right at me, he didn't seem to see me. "Pheebes?"

"I'm not Phoebe," I said, my head still down, my voice almost a whisper.

His arms fell to his sides. He stared at me, shook his head, and took a step backwards. The bed behind him caught him at the knees and he sat down hard. I watched. I wasn't sure what to do. If I stayed still, he might forget me. That was how it worked with Gran. When she was angry, it was like a whirlwind tearing through her. Once the rage passed, she seemed to forget about me unless I moved and caught her attention, and then she might come after me again. As long as I stood still, I was invisible. Her mind moved on to other things, and she'd walk away.

Maybe it would work the same way with Francis. Maybe if I didn't move, he'd lean back on the bed and go to sleep. Then I'd be able to figure out what to do—grab what I could and leave.

Instead, he said, "Not Phoebe?" as if this was the biggest mystery in the world.

He caught my wrist and pulled me closer, examining me, his face right up against mine. Then I could tell it was booze I smelled on his breath. "Not Phoebe," he said again flatly. I was waiting for him to let go of me, lie down and fall asleep so I could get out of there. And go where?

He let go of my arm and sagged on the edge of the bed, his head in his hands. He sat slumped over this way for a while. Then he straightened up, rubbed his eyes with the heels of his hands, ran a hand down his face. He looked at me. His mouth tightened in a grimace. "Of course you're not Phoebe."

He stood up and went and sat on the other side of the bed with his back to me. "Sorry if I scared you. If you want," he said in an empty voice, "I can take you back to Toronto tomorrow, drop you there. If you're uncomfortable," he added. He lapsed into silence for a moment, then continued, "I'd rather not, but I can't guarantee this won't ever happen again." He said over his shoulder, "I wasn't going to hurt you, Frankie. You know I'd never hurt you, don't you?"

He seemed older, diminished and shrunken. Defeated.

"Yeah, I know," I said. Because I felt this.

We stayed like that for a while, him sort of deflated, me perched on the side of the bed farthest from him.

After a while he said, "How about we sleep on it?" in a tired voice. "You can tell me in the morning what you want to do. I'll go sleep in the truck tonight."

"Okay," I said. "Sure."

The next day when I woke up, the sun was out. Francis knocked and came into the room. "Gotta brush my teeth," he said. "My mouth tastes like the bottom of a bird cage." He disappeared into the bathroom and came out with a toothbrush in his mouth. "How you doing?" he asked around the toothbrush and toothpaste.

I looked at him. "Okay, I guess."

"Ready to get moving?" he asked, sounding like his old self.

"All right." I figured I'd see how things went.

He flirted with the waitress at the restaurant, told me I could have whatever I wanted on the menu for breakfast, and rolled his eyes when I said what about ice cream. "Sure, ice cream for breakfast, if it's what you want," he said. He whistled as we checked out and hummed as we walked to the truck. Then, when we were sitting in the truck and ready to leave, he turned and asked me where I wanted to go—should he take me back to Toronto, or did the open road beckon? I told him I'd decided to stay. He nodded and started the engine. We never mentioned that night again.

6.

THAT WAS A COUPLE OF MONTHS AGO. Since then, we've been heading east. The country is more hilly here, the road swoops and dives. It's overcast, the whole sky a dull, even grey, but glowing somehow, so it hurts your eyes if you look at it too long. Francis is wearing his dark glasses.

It's one of those days seesawing on the edge between late winter and spring. Still a chill in the air but you can feel the energy stirring, making the buds on the trees unfurl into ragged gold-green leaves. I feel itchy, restless.

He's working on a loose schedule; we keep to the back roads until we have enough inventory, then, when we do, the game changes. Yesterday we stumbled on an estate sale in the middle of nowhere, an old stone farmhouse with its contents dragged out onto the lawn. Francis picked up what he called "fine specimens of early Canadiana," a dinged-up old wooden chest and a pile of quilts that looked pretty threadbare to me. We loaded them into the trailer and last night it was hard to find the space to drop the bunks.

This morning Francis started shifting gears. Before we hit the road, he examined his appearance in the truck's side-view mirror, rubbed his jawline. "Time to get spruced up," he said. "Shave and a haircut, two bits," a snippet of some old song I figure.

Now we're headed to some rinky-dink place—Elora? Elmira? He pointed out on the map in a general way where it is. I'm not sure how he decides where we're going, what his selection method is. I'm sure he'll tell me someday—he loves to talk. Some of the towns we stop in, it's clear he has contacts.

There's a place around here I recall from a few months ago, a small town we stopped in on our way somewhere else. I know we were near Guelph. I remember wondering out loud where the name Guelph came from. That was a mistake—I ended up getting a history lesson about tree-chopping and crazy kings. "You really should be in school, young lady," he said at one point.

"Not if this is what I'd have to listen to."

That night we checked into a motel. We got a unit with two rooms, like the one in St. Catharines—a bed in one room, a couch and a huge flat screen TV in the other. Francis took the TV room. As I drifted off, I could hear some program muttering in the background.

I woke up later and somehow knew right away Francis wasn't there. I checked the clock radio on the small bedside table; it said 10:23, so not too late.

I climbed out of bed and peeked into the other room. It was empty. The TV was on, still murmuring, but Francis was gone. There was this flash of heat—fear: had Francis dumped me and taken off the way my mom and dad had? On some level I'd assumed he wouldn't do that—perhaps I'd been wrong. Why would Francis be any different?

I tried to figure out what I'd tell the front desk in the morning if he didn't show up. Maybe it made sense to try and sneak out now.

I decided to see if the truck and trailer were still in the parking lot—that would mean he was still around. I pulled on my jeans and jacket, propped the door to the room open with the motel's welcome binder, tiptoed down the hall to the side exit, and peeked outside. The truck sat at the far end of the lot, right where we'd left it. So where was Francis? Then a movement caught my eye. Across the street was a small restaurant, what Francis would call a *greasy spoon*. It had a neon sign in the window with "Open" blinking on and off, except the letter "n" didn't light up, so the sign read "Ope." The interior of the place glowed brightly against the darkness.

There were people inside, several sitting at a counter, and one couple walking to a table in a corner, as far away from the counter as they could get. The man was walking behind the woman. I couldn't see her clearly, only enough to know she was slender and had long, fair hair. I could tell Francis by his walk, and when they reached the table, he pulled out a chair for her with a flourish—the kind of theatrical gesture I'd seen him make before when he was in a playful mood.

As I watched, the woman sat down and Francis took the seat opposite her. He waved to the waitress and held up two fingers. Then he turned his attention back to the woman. It looked like he asked her a question, then had to lean forward to hear what she said. She sat slumped in her seat with her chin tucked in, drawn into herself.

He said something to her; she shifted, sat up straighter. He said something else—this time she laughed, her head tipping up, her shoulders lifting, and he leaned back in his chair as if some unease between them had evaporated and he could relax.

I stood there for a few minutes, long enough to see her clasp her hands in front of herself on the table, to see him reach out and rest one of his hands on hers. The waitress arrived with mugs and menus, Francis and the woman slouched back in their chairs. The waitress handed them each a menu and I saw Francis look up at her, tip his head sideways as he asked a question. The woman looked up at the waitress, too. The three of them seemed to be chatting and kidding around. I wondered who the woman was—his ex-wife? A girlfriend? I stepped inside and went back to the room and to bed.

~

That was then, and here we are, back in the same general area. The Mennonites and their black horse-drawn buggies alert me.

Today is Thursday. We often roll into town around the middle of the week, because most of the time the antique market isn't open that early in the week and it gives us time to check out the place. I say *roll into town,* but it's more like we sneak. We ease our way in along the outskirts and when we're close enough to downtown, he parks on a side street.

Today he pulls up on a street lined with old grey stone houses that seem bleak and cold under the cloudy sky. We climb out and he locks the truck. Then we amble along the street, heading toward the middle of town. He carries a map (not a map of the town—we haven't had a chance to pick one up yet—but to someone who didn't know, it would look like we have one) and we behave the way tourists do. Stopping and starting, pausing in front of any interesting-looking building, pointing out unusual details to each other, inspecting the map, and wandering on.

I can tell we're getting closer to downtown when the touristy shops start to spring up, cutesy places selling what he calls useless pieces of gimcrackery. We walk into one, poke around. He picks something up, waves it in the air. "Come see this," he calls across the store. I wander over and examine a sculpture made of tiny shells glued together. We chat in low voices. An observer would assume we were talking about buying a souvenir. "The junk these places sell," he says in a low voice. "It's amazing they stay in business." He makes a big show of setting it back on the shelf so no one will suspect shoplifting. "Thanks," I call as we go out the door. Francis waves.

We're getting a feeling for the town. Each place has a different atmosphere. Some are cheerful; some are somber. We test the air, gauge the mood. A few months back, we washed up in a town that was grim and dreary, as if a cloud was permanently stalled over it. The residents looked grumpy and mean. The air felt thick and heavy, and a current of sourness ran through the place. After ten minutes we climbed back in the truck and drove away.

But we explore this town for a while and decide it feels okay, so the next step is finding a place to sleep, a base for operations. It's not cool to sleep in the trailer over night when we're in a small town. It draws attention. There have been times we've had what Francis calls *the strong arm of the law* or, when he's in a testy mood, *some rent-a-cop security minion* knocking on the trailer door in the middle of the night to inform us we're not allowed to stay in the grocery store parking lot all night, please move along. In these cases, a motel or B&B—anywhere we can land if he's too tired to keep driving—is a necessary expense.

Today we find a B&B close to downtown run by Mrs. Evans, an older woman who has a brisk manner, and salt and pepper hair pulled back into a tidy bun. She wears a white blouse buttoned all the way up, a dark green wool cardigan buttoned all the way down, and a tweed skirt. Francis pulls out his ID, I pull out my (fake) ID that proves I'm his flesh and blood, and she signs us in and makes it clear breakfast will only be served from 7:30 to 8:30 the next morning. *No exceptions*, she says, lowering her chin and looking at us over the tops of her glasses to emphasize her point.

We park the truck and trailer around the back of the B&B and unload our luggage: his bag, my knapsack. We each take a shower, he shaves, and then we go looking for someplace to eat.

Francis likes places with waitresses. He says talking to them is doing research. I say it's flirting. He says, "None of your lip," but he's grinning.

"Hey, Erma," he says to the middle-aged woman who shows up to take our order, reading her name off her nametag. "How you doing? This is my daughter, Eve. It's her birthday today, so I want to get her a special treat. What's the best thing on the menu? What do you recommend?" Even the surliest ones warm up to a man taking his daughter out for a birthday treat.

Erma has what Francis calls a *cool demeanor*. I'm sure there are guys trying to charm her like this all the time. She asks how old I am. I tell her I'm turning 17—which is true, just not this year. Francis says, "And you look young enough to be her sister."

Erma rolls her eyes at this, but I can see her warming up. She says the breakfast special is the best deal, and it's on all day.

"Any sights to see around here?" Francis asks. "What can you recommend?"

She rattles off a boring-sounding list: a church, town hall, some heritage building.

"How about antiques?" he asks. "They're a specialty of mine—" he breaks it up into five syllables, spe-ci-a-li-ty "—a little hobby. Anything local? Antique market?"

"There's one on Sunday," Erma says. "In the square in front of City Hall."

"Good to know," he says, then turns to me. "So, what does the birthday girl want to order?"

I get the breakfast special with white toast and scrambled eggs. Francis says, "Make that two, please. Over easy for me, and brown toast." He hands back the menu and beams at her. Now we know how many days we'll be hanging around here, how much time there is for us to make some connections.

At the end of the meal Erma brings us each a slice of chocolate cake with a dollop of vanilla ice cream on the side. The staff crowd around the table and sing "Happy Birthday." I act surprised and embarrassed. I *am* embarrassed.

We leave the restaurant and set about tracking down the bona fide antiquers—not the people who run faux-antique shops on the main street for tourists, but the people who know where the real goods are, who know when the auctions happen, and who frequent the estate sales. The folks who know an authentic Victorian washbasin when they see one, who can tell a genuine antique butter bowl from a knock-off. We ask around, learn their locations, some in low-slung warehouses on the outskirts of town where the rent's cheap, some a fair distance further out.

We're looking for the ones who sell at the market. We go in and out of several stores looking for someone who can point us in their direction. One shop is high-end—"A mite ritzy for our needs," Francis says. Another smells dank and fusty, and many of the items in it are worn and grimy, not a positive sign. Finally, we walk into a modest, welcoming store tucked away on a side street. There's an attractive sandwich board on the sidewalk beside the door with "Thanks for the Memories" expertly hand-painted in grey-blue and wheat on a cream background. The front window is artfully arranged: beautiful objects, but nothing too expensive or valuable, arrayed to show off each piece to best advantage. Francis stops in front of it and examines the display. After a moment he leans over and says in a low tone, "We're going to go in and do some research, you and me." Then his eyes lock on mine, his expression serious. "No sticky fingers—" he enunciates each word clearly"—got it?"

"No sticky fingers," I repeat. He nods.

When we walk in, there's a woman standing behind the counter on the right. She glances up when she hears the door open.

"May I help you?" she asks. She has a pleasant, quiet voice.

"My name's Joe Wilson," he says. "My daughter Mary Margaret and I—" he eases sideways a smidge so she can see me, "we're passing through town." I'm surprised he tells her my real name—well, not my *real* real name, but the closest to real one.

Her eyes move from him to me—they seem to snag on me for a second, then she looks back to Francis.

She's younger than him, maybe mid-thirties is my guess, although it's hard to tell. Her face is youthful-looking and smooth, but her hair is silver and pulled back into a long braid that hangs down her back. She inclines her head but doesn't respond. She seems reserved, like it would take a while to get to know her.

"Great shop you have here," he says, glancing around. He gives me a little shove—*get lost*—and continues talking to her. I fade, drift towards the back of the shop, as if I'm curious about what's back there, but the place is small enough I can hear their conversation. "Excellent quality merchandise," I hear him say. There's a tone in his voice, almost as if he's teasing her.

"Thank you," she says.

"Looks like business is booming."

"It's not bad."

"You must know some of the local folks, the antiquers," he says. He explains what he's looking for.

"Oh, you'd want Ray Cooper," she says. "He's had a stall on Sundays for decades. He's sort of out of the way..." She tells Francis where this guy lives, then there's a moment's pause. She reaches into a drawer. "Here, give him my card and tell him I sent you."

I move farther back and investigate the shelves along the back wall—a variety of different pieces, all in fine condition. I find a beautifully-crafted inkpot made of some metal—brass?—but constructed so it looks like it's woven out of wicker. It rests solidly in my palm and has a satisfying heft to it. There's a hinged lid that flips up to give access to the glass inkwell and shuts when it's not in use. On top of the lid, in relief, a crab sits above fishes swirling in a circle. A miniature frog clings to one side of the pot, a tiny crab to the other. How long before she'd notice if I slipped it into my pocket? She might not assume it was me, anyway—it's so portable anyone could walk off with it. Lifting the inkpot would be easy, and keeping it hidden from Francis wouldn't be difficult, but then I think about how upset Gran would be if she knew I was considering stealing it. Taking it not because Francis told me to—which I don't think she'd understand but that's the deal between him and me—but because I want it, and if I do it once, it'll probably be easier to do it the next time, which is the path to perdition she's always going on about. The thought freezes me for a second. And that's when I hear him say loud enough for me to hear, "Time to go." I give the pot a last look, put it back on the shelf, and join him at the front door.

As we're leaving, Francis calls, "Thank you kindly." We're half-way out the door when the hair on the back of my neck prickles. I peek back over my shoulder. The woman stands motionless behind the counter, watching us intently.

We return to the B&B, go around the back to the trailer. Francis unlocks the trailer door and disappears inside. When he comes out, he's carrying a scuffed and worn leather valise. We unhitch the trailer and set out in the pick-up, following the woman's directions. Half an hour later, down a winding country road, we come over the rise of a hill and find an old barn set back from the road the way she said we would. A weathered wooden sign, with "Cooper's Antiques" painted on it in fading letters, hangs on the end of the barn facing the road.

The barn looks locked up tight, but further back, up a narrow driveway that climbs a hill—two grooves worn into the earth—sits a large farmhouse.

We pull up on a muddy, grassy space maybe ten meters from the side door of the house. Just as Francis is unbuckling his seatbelt, there's the sound of a door banging and a tall, solid man comes out of the house, a cell phone to his ear, and waves for us to come up. He has a deep, carrying voice I can hear from where I sit in the truck, and a wide, sunburned face. As we get closer, I see he's nodding at whoever's on the other end of the line. He throws us a smile, points at his cell and holds up a finger to indicate he'll be with us in a minute. After a short conversation he hangs up and slips the phone into his pocket. "What can I do for you?" he asks.

"I'm looking for Ray Cooper," Francis says.

"Well, you found him," the man says, smiling and holding out his hand.

"My name's Joe Wilson," says Francis, shaking Ray's hand. "And this is my daughter, Frankie." He pauses, pats his pockets, pulls out the card the woman in the store gave him. "The woman from Thanks for the Memories gave us your name. She said to tell you she sent us."

Ray takes the card, nodding. "She's a good egg," he says. "Come on in." We follow him into a mudroom.

Ray drops the card Francis gave him on a sideboard inside the door. Francis slides his shoes off and indicates I should take mine off, too.

I trail after him and Ray into a spacious kitchen, a sunny room with lots of windows, warm after the day's chill, smelling of toast and lemon dish detergent.

There's a large pine table at one end of the room with piles of paper scattered all over it. Ray pushes the papers to one side and motions for us to sit down. "What can I get you? Coffee? Tea?"

"Coffee, thanks," says Francis.

Ray looks at me. "Coffee, please," I tell him, sitting down beside Francis.

There's lots of family pictures pinned to the fridge with magnets. Paintings and photos hang on the walls—odd bits and pieces, not necessarily pretty, that must have meaning to the people who choose to look at them every day. A brightly-coloured rag rug lies on the floor. The place is orderly, everything clean and polished. The furniture is old and shows signs of use—a nick here, a stain there. It looks like it's been around for a while, passed down through the family.

This isn't a room you'd ever find in one of those glossy, up-market interior decorating magazines I come across at the B&Bs, nestled among the piles of out-of-date gossip and lifestyle publications. This room is crowded and lived-in, with unmatched furniture and clutter, a place real people inhabit. I can imagine being far away and thinking of this room and remembering walking through the door into its jumble and comfort, how a warm feeling of anticipation would settle on you, a feeling like happiness or contentment at the thought of being home.

Ray pours us each a mug of coffee and sets a plate of cookies in front of us, then he pours a mug for himself and stands leaning against the counter. "You said Pascale sent you."

"She told us you have a stall at the antiques market," Francis says. "I'm on my way out west. I lost my wife—" his voice cracks. I watch him give Ray the same story he gave the woman at the Christmas rummage sale. Again, if I didn't know it was a performance, I'd totally believe him. "I brought a few items along," he finishes. "Can I show them to you?"

"That's rough." Ray says sympathetically. He sits down, leans back in his chair. "Sure, let's take a look. Bring them in."

Francis stands up. I sense him glancing at me, as if he wants me to follow him, but I look away. I'd rather stay in this warm, bright room. I hear the door shut behind him as he goes outside.

"Frankie," Ray says, pushing the plate of cookies closer to me. "That's an unusual name."

"It's really Frances, but I go by Frankie." I take another cookie.

"I see," he says, sipping his coffee. We sit in silence until Francis comes back carrying the leather valise.

He sets it on the table, unzips it, and pulls out Jean's paperweight, which he holds up for Ray to see. "Italian," he says, turning it over and setting it in Ray's hand. "See?" Points at the name etched on the base. "We bought it on our honeymoon, at a dingy little place in Florence. Hole in the wall." He shakes his head sadly at the memory.

Ray asks how much he wants for it.

"How much?" Francis repeats. "Oh..." He squints, does a quick calculation. "I want at least twenty—and you need your cut. And look, there's this..." So it goes, Francis pulling out one object after another, handing over each item, along with its story: a wedding gift, a birthday present. Every item has some sentimental weight to it. He has an infinite supply of these stories.

Ray examines the last article Francis hands him, a silver bowl with a Chinese scene embossed on it. He purses his lips and sets it on the table. "Nice," he says. "I could take a few of these, buy them off you if you want, or take them on consignment."

"I think consignment's better," Francis says. "You might be able to dicker the price up."

"That I might," Ray laughs. "Why don't you make a list—no, two—one for me and one for you—write down how much you want for each item. Bring it with you to the stall on Sunday, and I'll take it from there." He stands up. "I'm going to get some lunch going. You two hungry?"

"Oh, I wouldn't want to impose," Francis says.

"I'd be glad to have you," Ray says. "No trouble at all. My wife is in England with her sister. I'm all on my lonesome. It can get boring."

"Thanks," Francis says, "but there's some business we need to take care of. I'll find you Sunday morning."

"I'm in the front row," Ray says. "Ringside seat."

"Right," says Francis, picking up the valise. "Thanks. Thanks a lot."

He's pretty chipper as we walk to the truck, confident things will work out, that Ray will move the items and we'll end up with what he calls *venture capital.* "Easy money for him," he says walking lightly, bouncing on the balls of his feet. "And he gets some unique items on his table."

The game, as Francis calls it, rarely goes south. I've only ever seen two people try to stiff him. Once, a woman he'd left some sterling silver flatware with claimed she hadn't sold any of the items he'd consigned to her; they must have been stolen when she wasn't looking, she told him.

After she said this, I saw the same expression he'd had when he slapped me, his mouth curving, his eyes cold. "Oh, really?" he said, his voice quiet and even. "I wonder whether you'd want to tell the cops the provenance of the fine sterling silver tea set you have over there." He indicated a set at the end of her table. "Real unusual it is. I've seen a few in my time, but never one like that. The coffeepot must have been custom made. And you're selling it dirt cheap. Wouldn't be too hard to ask a few questions in the right places." He cocked his head and stared at her, raised his eyebrows.

Her face went white. She mumbled something about how she'd only this instant remembered the couple who'd come along mid-morning, and after them she'd got swamped; the sale slipped her mind until that very moment. She counted the bills into his hand.

"Thank you," he said, smiling for real this time. "Much appreciated. Pleasure doing business with you."

The other time it was a big, burly fellow. When we talked to him in the morning before the market opened, he seemed agreeable enough, but when we turned up later to collect our money, his eyes turned steely. I was suddenly aware of his bulk, how he loomed over Francis.

"How'd it go?" Francis walked up to him all friendly and cheery.

The man stared at him, expressionless. "Who the hell are you?" he asked, his voice level, dead.

Francis had left a set of Denby bowls, a Waterford vase, and a couple of cranberry glass candy bowls with him. We were going to have to walk away from several hundred dollars' worth of inventory.

Francis took in the man's humourless expression, his bunched muscles, and shrugged. "Right," he said, and turned and moved away. "Come on, Frankie," he murmured, reaching for my hand. I fell into step beside him.

Later, over coffee, he said, "You have to know when to walk away. There's not one thing in that trailer worth getting the shit kicked out of you for. It's nothing more than baubles and bibelots." Money was tight for a few days afterwards—there was instant oatmeal for breakfast, cup-a-soup for lunch and dinner—but we toughed it out.

~

He's cheerful and upbeat saying goodbye to Ray Cooper, but when we get closer to the truck, his mood flips— "What was that all about?" he demands. He grabs my arm, then glances past me at the house and lets go.

"What?" I ask, startled.

"Get in." He pushes me toward the passenger door, circles the truck, and climbs in on his side.

Then his hand is on my wrist again. "If I get up and leave, you get up and leave. No hanging around on your own. No answering strangers' questions."

I jerk my arm away and rub my wrist. "I knew you were coming back. I thought it would look weird if I went out with you and came right back. And all he did was ask my name."

"What'd you tell him?"

"My name is Frances and I go by Frankie."

"Well, you let me be the judge of what looks weird," he growls, turning the key in the ignition. "You just stay close."

But even as I sit beside him in the truck, part of me stands apart from him; I'm back in that warm, bright room with the trappings of family life all around.

~

Sunday's a clear day, sunny, with a faint breeze, warm enough for me to leave the winter parka he gave me in the trailer and put on the deep-pocketed hoodie—one of the first things he bought me. Francis always wears his beaten-up black leather jacket. It looks a hundred years old. "Unprepossessing," he calls it. I call it mangy. He says it gives him a negotiating advantage. "If you look like you have money, people drive a harder bargain than if you look like you're barely scraping by."

Bright and early, even before Mrs. Evans is up, we walk down to the market and find Ray Cooper's stall.

"Hey, how you doing?" he says, standing and holding out his hand to Francis when we arrive. He seems genuinely glad to see us. He puts down what he's holding, a green ivy butterdish.

"Good, good." Francis says. He sets the valise on Ray's table and starts unloading items: the old lady's paperweight, the silver bowl he showed Ray before, a pair of matched silver candlesticks, a Wedgwood jug, and a cloisonne art deco vase, and a few more. None of them big, all fine quality.

"Great," says Ray, picking up the Wedgwood jug and examining it.

"Here's the list." Francis passes him a sheet of paper. Ray skims it, nodding. "Looks reasonable. Are you sure you only want thirty for the candlesticks?" He picks one up and checks the bottom. "I ought to be able to get twice that, easy."

"Any amount over what I put down, we split the surplus sixty-forty in your favour. Sound good?" Francis says. "Incentive for you to get the most you can."

Ray laughs. "I like that arrangement." Then he gives the table a slap. "All right," he says, "so we'll see you around four."

"Okay," says Francis, and we wander away.

First, we eat. We find the cheapest place we can and order bacon and eggs. Then we go back to the market, steering well clear of Ray's booth.

We've done this so many times we don't even discuss it, it's become automatic: he goes in one direction around the market, and I go in the opposite direction. We dawdle from stall to stall. At this stage I rarely pick anything up; I'm scoping out what's available, making mental notes. It takes twenty minutes for me to work halfway around the perimeter. We step away from the market, meet up at a predetermined point—in this case, back at the greasy spoon where we ate—and exchange information.

"Third booth from the start," I tell him. "Have a look at the coins."

"Check out the guy with the John Deere baseball cap," he says. "It might be a real ivory comb he has there." He rattles off a few more items, then he says, "We'll meet at the coffee place at the corner of King and Main in about half an hour, okay?" He leaves first. I wait a couple of minutes before moving on.

When I've finished the second half of the walk-around I head to the coffee shop. He buys us each a coffee, and we sit at a table and compare notes. "The John Deere guy," he says, "skip the comb—too big. There's an ivory thimble. That's what you're after." He tells me which items he's really interested in at what booths, and which ones to aim for if I can't get the top-flight ones. Then we split up again and head back to the market separately. He heads for the pieces he really wants, the challenging ones that are fairly valuable. I aim for the smaller ones.

I move from table to table, picking up items, examining them, then setting them back down again. Once in a while, to make it look authentic, I pull out my wallet and count through the cash Francis gave me, as if I'm checking to see if I have enough to buy what I have my eye on. Disappointed, I tuck it back in my pocket and move on. The cash is also useful because if I get nabbed, I can prove I meant to buy the item, I simply forgot to pay.

At one booth, the woman running it catches me looking at a piece. "Oh, that's a lovely Blue Mountain vase," she says. "You don't see that style often."

I smile and say, "Yeah, it's memorable," but Francis has told me, "Whatever you do, never—*never*—pick up any Blue Mountain crockery. It's impossible to move." Most of the time I fly under the radar and avoid talking to people, but it's funny, if you do that too much, if you're trying too hard to be inconspicuous, it draws attention the same way being too conspicuous does—it sets off alarm bells. So, if someone talks to me, I engage, maybe I tell them it reminds me of something my gran had. The past tense and my solemn expression, the way my chin crumples, often cut the conversation short.

The objects I'm after are items I can slip into my pocket. At the John Deere guy's booth, I manage to nick the thimble painlessly. Then I leave the market and, in a winding, leisurely way, checking over my shoulder once in a while to be sure no one is following, I wander back to the trailer and unload it, using the key he gave me a couple of weeks ago. "Because now you're a trusted assistant and all that."

Over the course of the morning I make three trips, one item at a time. "Don't be greedy," he's said. "Better to end the day empty-handed than in the hands of the law."

He's doing the same. Sometimes we bump into each other at the trailer, mostly we don't.

~

As the day goes on, it gets warmer. The breeze settles down. For lunch we grab sandwiches from a deli and walk back to the trailer.

"One more go-round," he says. "And then we're done for the day. Fun and games until it's time to collect our money and leave."

We return to the market. Vendors are bringing out new inventory to replace what they've sold, items Francis and I haven't seen before. If we've had a profitable haul in the morning, we're not likely to lift any more articles in the afternoon, but it's always worth finding out what's on offer.

At the stall beside the Blue Mountain lady (the vase is still there), I find a cigarette case I haven't seen before, an elegant silver box with a design etched into the cover. I pick it up. It has a pleasing weight to it. The design is Art Deco, I think, some curving lines but not as fluid as Art Nouveau. I bring the case closer, trying to decipher the initials I see woven into the centre of the curling lines. A wasp buzzes past; I wave my hand to sweep it away, and that's when I become aware of—feel, rather than see—a shape I suddenly recall sensing earlier, a blot of darkness on the day's brightness. The hairs on the back of my neck stand up.

I put the cigarette holder down and pick up a slim silver penknife lying beside it. I don't want to leave too quickly—it might alert whoever is following me that I'm onto them. Better to behave as if I don't know I'm being watched.

I set down the penknife and move away, toward another table Francis suggested I look at. Once there, I scan my surroundings surreptitiously, but nothing and no one out of the ordinary register, it's all business as usual.

When I find Francis a few minutes later, he asks, "How'd you do?"

"No luck this time around."

"Luck has nothing to do with anything," he says tersely. "If that's all you ever learn from me, I've done you a service."

"I think someone was following me."

He gives me a speculative look. "You should have come and found me, but no worries." He waves his hand carelessly. "We're heading out. I collected from Ray. Had a superlative day. No more markets for a while. Let's get moving."

Back at the B&B we pack up the truck and hit the road. Between when we left the market and when we get on the road, it feels like the temperature's changed. Francis seems to be in a better mood, humming a bouncy, upbeat song, more at ease, some edge gone.

"Made some calls, made some plans," he says. "Got places to go, things to do." We're heading out of town, toward the highway. He's full of energy, talkative, he wants to chat. "Did I ever tell you how I started in the business?" he asks.

"You never tell me anything about your life," I say.

"Oh, that's not true, Frankie," he says in a half-scolding, half-sad tone. "I've told you lots. My life is an open book to you."

7.

"WHEN I WAS TWELVE," HE SAYS, "the circus came to town, and when they left, I ran away with them. There aren't many travelling circuses left, which is a tragedy. They were useful for separating those of us who wanted adventure from our families, who wanted us to stick to the straight and narrow." He grins.

We're driving through the outskirts of town, past the adult stores, the tattoo parlours, the tawdry motels.

Francis tells me about the circus, how the smells of the midway were what hooked him first: spun sugar, popcorn and butter, engine grease. There was also the smell of manure, he mentions. And the sounds—people shouting, the machinery creaking and grinding, a recording of a calliope tune looping over and over, the noises the animals made.

He tells me how he snuck away from home in the middle of the night ("No love lost there," he says) and showed up at the circus while the roustabouts were pulling down the tents and packing up the trailers.

"It was the elephants I was interested in," he says. "They were enormous. And they watched you—observed you, really—with eyes that looked human. I could tell there was an intelligence in there. We only needed some way to connect."

He sidled up to the elephant trainer, who looked at him

with narrowed eyes, then shrugged, and said, "You'll have to sleep in the truck."

While he's telling me this, the city dissolves into suburbs, and then the suburbs thin out into country: back roads with no apparent names, stretches where trees crowd up to the edge of the road and not much else is visible, only a house or a farm once in a while through a gap in the forest.

I don' t know if I believe him, but here's the thing about Francis: it doesn't matter if you believe him or not, the stories are always entertaining.

The elephant man's real name was Rockwell Jones, but everyone called him Lucky because he had a bad eye, a bad leg and—rumour had it—deep in his past, a love affair gone wrong.

"Mamie and Rosie," Francis says, "they were his girls and he loved them like daughters. Slept in the trailer with them, had a sheet of plywood that made a separate space big enough for a mat and a sleeping bag for him, so if something happened—if there was a thunderstorm and they got spooked, or if some goof came around looking for trouble—he was right there.

"He knew all there was to know about them, more than the folks at the border did. We'd be crossing from the US into Canada, and the guys at the border wouldn't know if Mamie and Rosie were African or Asian, male or female, but Lucky could tell you practically to the ounce what went in and what came out. He was always massaging them, talking to them.

"The reason he took me on was his last assistant had a little too much to drink one night and crawled into the girls' trailer to sleep it off. You don't, as a rule, position yourself underfoot of an elephant, especially in the dark." Francis shakes his head. "Not that Rosie or Mamie meant to hurt him, it's just that elephants are near-sighted and when he stumbled in, he spooked them. Lucky said Rosie and Mamie were pretty upset when it happened.

It took him a long time to settle them."

Saturnine is the word Francis uses to describe Lucky. "As in the planet Saturn," he says, when I look at him, puzzled. "As in serious, as in having a gloomy, grave or melancholy character," he explains. "As in not jolly. See how I'm expanding your vocabulary?"

Lucky wasn't loquacious, as Francis put it. "A couple of words would usually do the trick, *no* being one of the more frequent ones, along with *fucking idiot*. He only used those for me, never for the girls. Never even raised his voice at them."

But Francis and Lucky got along in their own way. "Mostly, I figure, because me and the girls got on well. I wasn't afraid of them, and they were fond of me, always tickling me with their trunks, or nipping me. What you need to know about elephants is, you have to be straight with them. You have to look them in the eye. Mess with them, they can tell. They can smell it, and it's a bad idea to screw around with an animal that weighs so much more than you."

He tells me about being on the road, going town to town, building up his list of contacts. "Which is how I met Eddy," he says. "We were at the Ex in Toronto, at the CNE, and there's this runty kid hanging around, his ears nearly as big as the girls' ears. So, I introduce myself and show him around. Fast friends ever since. One of these days you'll meet Eddy."

Francis stayed with Lucky for a couple of years. Then Rosie became sick—"She was no spring chicken"—and when she died, Lucky followed her soon after. "Broken heart, is what I think," Francis says. "He loved those girls. After she was gone, I watched the life drain right out of him. He grew quieter and quieter. He'd been a huge guy—over three hundred pounds—but by the end he was down to nearly nothing. Then he was gone."

Mamie had a hard time, but she was a trouper, he says. He

and she kept each other going. "We heard about another cow looking for a home. I went and checked her out, thought she'd be a good fit. That's how Tiny came to us." For eight years they travelled around. "I even found myself an assistant," he says. "Tony DeMarco. A smart kid. He's still at it today."

One day the circus stopped in a small town in Kentucky. "Gorgeous place. Poor as stink, but incredibly beautiful." They got ready for the show and the set-up was going smoothly. "Too smoothly. Should have known, shouldn't I?" It's not really a question. Or, if it is, he's not asking me.

"I thought I knew what I was doing, thought everything was under control. Mamie, Tiny, and I were making our entrance, and I looked up. Only a glance, could just as easily not have happened. And right there, ringside, is the most beautiful girl I have ever seen. Knocked the wind right out of me. She had long, blonde hair, like light falling over her shoulders, and cool grey eyes. She was like a magnet, my eyes kept being drawn to her. She knew it, too. And it looked like she was laughing at me."

He says it was his own fault, what happened next. "Should have been paying better attention."

Mamie went up into her headstand. "I should have had my eye on her," he says, "but I didn't. She came down—right on my leg."

The instant it happened, people started screaming. Mamie tried to back away. "People figured she was trying to step on them. They jumped up and started running, shouting. Some people were rushing at Mamie and Tiny, waving. I'm calling for Tony to get the girls out of there, away from the noise and the panic. If they freaked out, the situation might get ugly."

Finally, Tony calmed the girls down and steered them out of the tent. Then people were clustering around "Asking damn fool questions, like, 'Where does it hurt?' 'Where do you think, asshole?' I wanted to say. I knew my leg was crushed. An elephant comes down on you, that's pretty obvious."

He passed out, and when he woke up, he was in a hospital bed. And sitting next to him was the girl with the golden hair.

"She looked at me when I woke up and smiled, only a little. I said, 'My name's Francis.' She said, 'So I gathered.' Then I ran out of conversation to make—for about the first time in my life—and I just lay there and looked at her. After a while I said, 'I bet not many men go to these lengths to chat with you.' Then she laughed and shook her head. 'You're right about that.' She had a voice like clear, cool water on a hot day. 'What's your name, then?' I asked. 'Tamsin,' she said. 'Your friends call you Tammy?' I asked. 'No,' she said. 'They call me Tamsin.'"

The doctors pinned his leg, but there was no way he was going to be able to go back in the ring, they told him. Another accident, even a minor one, and with all the damage done, they couldn't guarantee anyone would be able to fix him up again. In that case, he might even lose the leg, they said.

"The circus had left while I was lying in bed. The show must go on and all that. Contracts to fulfill. I lay there wondering what I was going to do, where I was going to go."

Tamsin came by every day or two. She'd show up with coffee and sometimes donuts. She'd sit by the bed and they'd chat. He told her about circus life. She told him about growing up dirt poor in a large, noisy family. As they grew better acquainted, he discovered that under her quiet, shy exterior she was really smart, and had a wicked sense of humour.

But she was there only an hour or so a day out of the dozens of hours, hundreds of hours he lay stretched out in bed.

One of the Ladies' Auxiliary volunteers—mid-sixties, maybe, short and round with a tendency to run off at the mouth—came by every few days pushing a rattling trolley full of scuffed, tired magazines and books, paperbacks mostly, with dog-eared pages and broken spines, the covers worn to softness from repeated readings, often smelling like someone's damp basement. To cut short her gabbing he'd grab a handful, thank her, hold one up, open it as if he couldn't wait to get started.

One of the magazines was a catalogue of antiques. Black and white pictures: crocks, bowls, jars, glassware. Yawn, he thought, about to put it down. Then a picture caught his eye, a shot of a bread-maker like the one his mother had had—an old tin bucket with a handle across the top that turned a crank in the bucket to knead the dough. His mother's had been dented and worn. He read the price listed beneath the picture and let out a low whistle. *That much*, he thought. Well, now, who'd have thought.

That was the beginning. He devoured the catalogue and asked the chatty volunteer for more. He asked Tamsin to find him books on antiques. She arrived with an armful from the town library. He read each one, cover to cover.

By the time he was discharged, he'd found a new vocation. He knew what he was going to do and he knew what he needed to do it.

He started small-scale. He had some money saved. (One precept Lucky had drilled into him was: no one's going to look out for you but you, so you'd better do a good job of it yourself, and he'd made Francis keep part of every paycheck. Francis stashed the cash in a money belt he never let out of his sight.) One of Tamsin's cousins, an auto mechanic, found a rusted beat-up half-ton. "It looked like hell, but this guy knew what he was doing, and when he was finished, it drove like a dream."

Francis began by visiting the hamlets and villages in eastern Kentucky, where Tamsin's aunts, uncles, and dozens of cousins once and twice removed lived. The places were gold mines; he bought old oil lamps for the price of a cup of coffee each, wired them up with an electric bulb shaped like a candle flame, and sold them to upscale tourist shops for ten times what he'd paid. Then the shops, in places like Louisville and Lexington, marked them up 100 percent and sold them to tourists, who liked the idea they were buying something authentic, something genuine. Win, win, win, Francis said. Everyone was happy.

He and Tamsin weren't an item at first, but as he continued to recover, "And as my natural charming self re-emerged, well, she couldn't resist," he says with a grin.

Francis found he was naturally suited to this line of work. "I'd picked up patter in the circus, learned how to grease the wheels of the sales process." Business was remunerative, he says; within a year he was able to buy a trailer, and with the help of Tamsin's cousin, remodel it. "I paid him to put two bunks in instead of one—always thinking ahead, see? Always optimistic, that's me. Then I asked her to marry me. Practically fell over when she said yes, pretty nearly exploded with happiness."

It was a modest ceremony, almost one year to the day after the accident. "My god, she was beautiful," he says. "A white lace wedding dress and white flowers in her hair. Couldn't take my eyes off her. The preacher had to ask me twice before I snapped out of it and said, 'I do.'"

He's more or less forgotten me. After a minute he blinks like he's waking up, looks at me briefly, then lets out a long breath.

"So where are they?" I ask.

"Who?"

"Tamsin and Phoebe."

An expression flits across his face really fast, not as simple as a frown. "Well, you can't raise a child on the road," he says. "We tried. For the first little while we took Pheebes with us—to markets, on house calls.

"She proved surprisingly useful. A baby shows up and all eyes are on it. Having her along made certain aspects of our work much easier, people were sympathetic to two young folks with a kid, they were more disposed to give us, let's call them, preferential deals."

But only while she was tiny, he continues. "Once she started walking, it became more complicated. She wasn't happy to just be quiet and cute. That was never Pheebes' way. She wanted to be exploring, and she'd put up a fight if we didn't let her."

He tells me they found a place in Vermont—the top floor of a house in a hamlet that wasn't much more than the intersection of two highways. "Tamsin grew up in a small town and she wanted her kids to grow up in one, too. She liked the mountains, the country."

It was in New England, where they'd built up a network of friends and contacts. And also close to Canada.

"The first time we visited Canada, I couldn't believe it," he says. "All these great old items—furniture, housewares—and no one wanted them. Hell, they'd pay us to take 'em away. They were all into this streamlined teak stuff. No one wanted the old pine chests, the rocking chairs. Getting it across the border was a lot easier then, too."

Bit by bit his business moved north of the border. "Eddy—remember I mentioned him before, from the circus—he turned me on to some people, and I ran into others." Then people started to get interested in their own history. "Funny how it works," he says. "What your parents owned is boring; what your grandparents owned is history." And Francis was there to sell it to them.

They moved to Canada and opened a shop. It was possible then. But as time passed, things changed.

"We didn't split up so much as drift apart, Tamsin and me." He sounds wistful, slightly sad. "I still see Tam. I drop in every few months." I suspect he's exaggerating how often he visits, because in the time I've been travelling with him he's never visited her, or made any noise suggesting he would.

"She met a fellow, a stand-up guy," he tells me. "A carpenter. He fixes up old houses."

"And Phoebe?"

"Oh, the kid's at uni. Like I told you—smart. Smarter than her old dad by a country mile."

"Why now?" I ask.

"What?"

"Why are you telling me this now?"

"Didn't know you well enough before," he says teasingly.

I guess it's an answer, but knowing him, it's not the whole answer.

~

The next morning, it's like he's reached a decision. He's more serious, less playful.

"Rise and shine," he says, shaking my shoulder to wake me up. No jokes, no goofing around. "Got your things?" he asks, scanning the room from the doorway.

"Yup."

"Let's go."

We pay the motel bill, gas up, and pull onto the highway.

"Showtime, folks," he says in a quiet voice.

"What?"

His gaze lands on me, then bounces away. "Nothing." He shakes his head. "Merely a saying." He starts humming a song I don't recognize. "We're going to Eddy's," he says. "These small-town dealers are all well and good for some quick cash, but Eddy has the big bucks."

He's made reference to a number of guys scattered around

in various cities: Eddy is in Toronto; Deluze is in Montreal; he's mentioned someone in Winnipeg a couple of times, and another guy in Halifax. But Eddy's the one he's mentioned most frequently.

"Does he know about me?"

"Who? Eddy?" he says, frowning. "No."

By the time we get to the eastern side of Toronto, it's getting dark. Francis phones Eddy from the highway. "I haven't eaten yet," he tells him. "I'm going to pick up some food. What do you want?"

Eddy suggests an East Indian place, so we buy enough for three and get back on the road. We drive through an industrial park. Most of the places are shut up tight, dark. There's one place we pass with a huge neon sign: Lougheed's Haulage, and soon after that we pull off the road, into what looks like a parking lot ringed by a chain link fence. The yard is about the size of a football field. Sitting in the middle of it is a lone rusted car, at the far end is a warehouse. Francis drives past the car toward the warehouse.

It's a derelict-looking building. If I were passing by on my own, I'd assume it was deserted. It's three stories tall and most of the windows are broken, some boarded up with sheets of plywood. The walls are covered in layers of graffiti. It looks impassive, closed. Then I notice one of the loading docks in the far corner is open. Francis drives straight towards it.

He steers the truck into the building and stops. Suddenly, shrieking and grinding, the loading dock door drops shut behind us. We sit in complete darkness.

A moment later, a door opens in the shadows in front of us. A bright shaft of light falls on the floor and a man walks through the light, into the space. Francis climbs down, I follow a few steps behind him.

The other guy is shorter than Francis, compact and muscular, sinewy. He has ink on his arms—an eagle, a wolf's head. Francis steps aside when I come up behind him and gestures for me to join them. "Eddy," Francis says, introducing us, "Frankie. Frankie, Eddy."

Eddy gives me the once over. "Hi," he says. He's younger than Francis, I'd guess, his voice even, quiet. His dark hair is buzzed short. There's a sleek, self-contained quality to him that reminds me of a cat. Before, Francis said something about Eddy's ears, but they look normal to me. Must be a Francis exaggeration.

"Come on in," Eddy says. We follow him through the door. On the other side is an office, plain: a desk, some chairs. One has a worn black vinyl seat cracked with age; someone's tried to mend it with duct tape but bits of stuffing poke out where it's ripped. There's a green filing cabinet and a fluorescent light overhead. We follow Eddy through the room, to a door in the wall behind the desk that opens onto a landing with a flight of stairs leading up. At the top of the stairs, Eddy unlocks a heavy metal door and we step into an apartment with soaring ceilings and polished wood floors. We're standing in what must be the living room, a wide, open space with a long leather couch on one side, a couple of chairs on the other, a glass and chrome coffee table between them, and a huge flat-screen TV off to one side. At the far end of the space is a kitchen area.

Francis whistles approvingly. "Not bad. Big changes since the last time I was here. Business must be okay."

"Can't complain." Eddy says. "So, where's this food you promised?"

I set the plastic bag from the Indian restaurant on the coffee table. Over dinner, Francis explains, "Eddy's in the import/export business." An ambiguous look passes between the two of them.

There's more talk. Time passes. I start to feel drowsy.

"You want to crash here tonight?" Eddy asks, when I try unsuccessfully to stifle a yawn for the third time.

"That'd be great," Francis says. "We can sort everything in the morning."

"You stretch out there," Eddy says to me, indicating the couch. He disappears and returns with a pillow and a blanket. Then he and Francis shift the chairs to the other side of the room.

As I drift between waking and sleeping, I catch bits and pieces of their conversation.

"What's with the girl?" Eddy asks at one point.

"Her? She's my get out of jail free card," Francis answers, chuckling. "She does the work—they can't touch me."

~

A grinding noise wakes me the next morning. I sit up, peer over the back of the couch, and see Eddy in the kitchen at the other end of the loft pouring water into a coffeemaker.

"Coffee?" he asks.

"Sure." I stand up and stretch, then wander down to that end of the space. Eddy looks over when I lean on the island that serves as a kitchen table.

"How'd you sleep?" he asks. He turns to fiddle with something on the stove. There's the smell of melted butter in the air, and a radio is on in the background with someone talking about traffic.

"Fine," I say. "Where's Francis?" I recall Francis's instructions about not answering strangers' questions.

"In the shower." He turns and pops two slices of bread in a toaster. "You want some breakfast?"

"I guess."

"So," he says, pouring a mug of coffee and handing it to me, then pouring himself one. "How long have you known Francis?"

I hesitate. What has Francis told him? How much can I say?

Noting my hesitation, Eddy waves the question away. "If you're not comfortable—" He turns around, opens the fridge and starts digging around in it.

"I don't know. Since last year."

"How'd you meet?" he asks from behind the fridge door. He pulls out a jug of milk and sets it on the counter.

"We. . .met. He said I reminded him of Phoebe."

His eyes flicker over to me, then he reaches for the sugar bowl and spoons some into his coffee. "He told you about her, did he?"

"Yeah. I'd like to meet her sometime. The way he talks about her..."

Eddy's quiet for a minute, then Francis walks into the room.

"Sweet place," he says, pulling a sweatshirt on over his head. "Nicely done."

"I'm trying to stay under the radar," Eddy says. "If a building inspector ever sees the place, I'll be shut down."

"So," Francis turns to me, "me and Eddy, we're going to do some horse trading this morning, right, Ed?" Grinning, he punches Eddy lightly on the shoulder. Eddy nods.

After we've eaten, the three of us go down to the first floor and through the office to the space where the truck and trailer are parked. Francis opens the trailer door and tells me to hop up. "Bring out the rocker," he says, "the one you said looked uncomfortable."

When he sees the rocker, Eddy whistles. "Nice," he says.

Over the next few hours, the two of them examine and dicker over some chairs, a chest, a set of flatware. ("Sterling silver," Francis says grandly. "Yeah, but nude mermaids?" Eddy replies, holding up a soup spoon and peering at the ornately decorated handle. "Okay," he sighs. "I think I know someone who might be interested.") A folding table decorated with fine marquetry patterns in geometric shapes, and a dozen or so more modest items.

"Missed a beautiful little table near Athens, remember, Frankie?" Francis shakes his head. "I couldn't figure out how to separate it from the granny who owned it."

"You didn't do too badly," Eddy says, looking at all the items piled on the floor. "That's a profitable haul."

"Right. Well," Francis rubs his hands. "Pay up, boyo, and we'll be off."

Eddy pulls a roll of bills out of his pocket, peels some off, and hands them to Francis. "Pleasure doing business with you," he says.

Without counting the bills, Francis deals me a few and tucks the rest into his inside jacket pocket. "Mutual, I'm sure," he says. Then, in a more serious tone, "Thanks, Ed."

"Stay away from those loose women," Eddy says to him. "And you—" pointing at me—"don't trust this guy any further than you can throw him."

"*Pfft.*" Francis says dismissively. He wraps his arm around my shoulders. "What are you talking about, Eddy? You know she's like a daughter to me." He gives my shoulders a squeeze. "A daughter."

Then he drops his arm from my shoulders, suddenly all business. "Right." He pats his pockets, fishes out his keys. "Delightful as this visit has been," he says to Eddy, "it's time for us to hit the road."

We climb into the truck. Eddy opens the loading dock door and we back out. I watch Eddy until the door slides down, cutting him off from sight. Once again, the building stares at us impassively. Francis turns the truck and trailer around. We drive out of the parking lot, the world in front of us is framed by the truck's window. Only me and Francis again.

"So, we did great with Eddy," Francis says. "I have some irons in the fire that require my attention. We're going to be staying in the Big Smoke for a couple of days." A friend of Eddy's has an apartment that needs looking after, he tells me. "We can crash there. Right downtown," he says. "Near your old haunts." The way he says this, the way his voice lands precisely on the last three words—as if he's teasing me—makes the phrase catch in my ears.

"Think of it as old-home week, except it'll be old-home couple of days."

It turns out the apartment is kind of funky, the second storey of a red brick building—Victorian-era, is my guess—on Queen Street West, just east of Spadina. The broad living room window looks south over Queen Street. The walls are painted wine-red, there are plants everywhere, a stained-glass panel above the front window, and a worn Oriental rug on the floor. Whoever lives here knows about art and antiques: there are remarkable artifacts (what Francis calls something when it's the real thing) scattered around: a life-sized sculpture of a Chinese child's face displayed on the mantelpiece over the fireplace; a delicate vase, about three feet high, with eggshell-thin walls, stands in one corner. There's a creepy painting on the wall. Francis sees me looking at it sideways. "That's a Burra," he says. "And over there—" he points to a collection of circles and shapes hanging from the ceiling and revolving slowly in the air "—is a Calder. That beauty is worth more than you or I are ever likely to have, unless we get lucky on the lottery."

He notices me looking at the Chinese sculpture. "No sticky fingers," he says. "Never shit where you eat, never steal from your host, got it?"

I think of the granny whose Italian paperweight I liberated. "Sure," I say, like *of course. I'm not stupid.*

"All right. Let's get settled."

He takes the master bedroom, I get the other, smaller bedroom, spare, simple, the walls painted a pale blue tone, the bed covered in a puffy white comforter. Standing in the middle of the room feels like being inside a cloud. I fall backwards onto the bed and lie, staring at the ceiling, imagining I'm falling up into the sky.

Francis calls, "Frankie."

I follow his voice down the hall to the kitchen. It's at the very back of the place, and runs the entire width of the apartment. There's an exposed brick wall, a stainless steel fridge, a serious gas oven—the kind professionals use—and lots of shiny copper pots hanging from a metal grid suspended from the ceiling, above an island in the centre of the room.

Francis is sitting at the island—a wide, heavy slab of wood planed to smoothness on top and treated with wax or varnish to give it a shine, the edges left rough and uneven with patches of bark intact. He has his cell out and is scrolling through it.

"Frankie, my darlin'," he says without looking up, "I have leads to follow up, deals to finalize, so you're going to be on your own for a while. Fortunately, I know you have the inner resources to handle being on your own." He reaches into his pocket, and tosses something that jangles across the table to me—keys. "I'll stock up the larder," he says, putting his phone down. "You can eat here if you want. I won't always be around, so help yourself when you need to. No visitors—understand?" he says sharply.

I nod.

"Okay." He picks up his cell and stands. "Gotta go." He points a finger at me. "No visitors."

"No visitors," I repeat.

He winks. I hear his footsteps going down the stairs, hear the front door open and close behind him, and I stand in the kitchen, alone for the first time in a long time.

I wander from room to room. It feels peculiar being in this empty, quiet space after being crammed into the truck so long with Francis, the radio tuned to Country and Western most of the time, spending nights in cramped motel rooms, or overstuffed B&B rooms, Francis always by my side or nearby. I feel weightless, floating, like I've lost or misplaced part of myself. I find my knapsack and pull out the picture of my mom—somehow, looking at it helps me feel more solid, more real.

After a while, though, I start to feel the itch of restlessness. In the front room, there's a wall with built-in bookshelves jammed with hundreds of books arranged in neat, tidy rows. I find one about Edward Burra and read about him, which leads me to Paul Nash, and then Stanley Spencer.

Every once in a while, I gaze down at the street and watch the people walking—some in a hurry to get to their destination, others simply ambling along—and for the first time since I met Francis, I feel lonely for the crowds of the city, which is odd, because there they are, right down there. Or maybe I recognize my loneliness for the first time, maybe it's been there all along and I didn't see it.

I want to be down there, walking around. I want to see if the city feels the way I remember.

I put the books back where they belong, go to my bedroom and grab my jacket, make sure I have the keys, and head downstairs. The door closes behind me. I turn east, recognizing the shops and storefronts from when I was on the street, before I met Francis. As I walk along, the neighbourhood seems different now from how it used to be, and at the same time, unchanged, as if there are two different cities, one layered over the other; the old one underneath, and the new one above it, floating over what I recall. Only sometimes I have such a vivid memory of a place, the old memory blots out any new impression I might have, so as I walk along there's a constant shift between what I remember and how the city looks to me now, and I don't feel like I'm fully in either time.

To my new eyes, the streets look narrower, on a smaller scale than I recall, and grittier, but at the same time, they're familiar, and there's a level of comfort in that.

Before—before Francis—what I cared about was finding food, and warm, dry, safe places to stay where people wouldn't come along and hassle me or tell me to move on. I'd walk along scanning the sidewalk for coins people had dropped and anything else valuable or useful. I had a map in my head of where I could go to get free food, where I could get out of the weather, safe spaces to sleep. I knew the dry places, and the dark places where I would never go alone. I knew all the public washrooms, the spots I could duck into if there was a sharp wind blowing, and I moved from one location to the next along a series of lines linking them.

In those days, the city was like a connect-the-dots map, and I kept travelling the same routes—the safe ones—without sight-seeing, my eyes fixed on the specific and the necessary.

Today, instead of being a set of distinct locations connected by lines, the city is more like a mosaic, a collection of colours, shapes, smells, and sounds that overlap and make a noisy, crowded, jumbled whole—not a web, but a messy, bustling landscape.

For the first time, I notice how, right near one of the shelters where I used to stay, there's an enormous glass greenhouse full of large-leafed tropical plants. I must have walked past the building dozens of times and never gone through the doors.

Inside, the air is warm and thick and smells *green*: of leaves and stems, of things growing and things rotting. Brightly-coloured flowers blink in and out of sight. Somehow a bird has found its way in and it flits past in sudden, stuttering bursts.

Another discovery: in the same block as one of the spots where I used to eat for free, there's now an oddball store, half avant-garde art gallery (the current show is some woman's selfies distorted into really disturbing pictures), half artsy bookstore: monographs (Francis explained what a monograph is; he claims it's part of him giving me an education, I say it's part of him liking the sound of his own voice), books, catalogues, art magazines. I know enough now that some of what I skim makes a little bit of sense to me, though not too much of it.

I guess when you're alone and scared and hungry, your vision narrows. You're predator and prey, both, and you only have enough time and energy for essential information: food, safety, warmth.

But when you don't have to focus on simply the basics, the world opens up as stranger and more complicated than it seemed when your main priorities were getting enough to eat and staying out of the cold.

I walk miles and miles, from the west side to the east side and back.

~

When I return to the apartment later, it's empty. But Francis must have been back already: there's food in the fridge, a loaf of bread on an otherwise empty counter, and a note: "Help yourself. I'll be late. See you in the morning. F."

There's no TV, but it doesn't matter. Gran never had one. She said it was the servant of Satan and Mammon. I didn't totally understand what she meant then, but judging from what I've seen in the motels Francis and I have stayed in, I'd have to agree. Satan, Mammon, and boredom. Lots of boredom.

I go to the bookshelves in the front room and pull down a book about an artist called Milton Avery. His paintings really do look like pictures a kid could make, like paper cut outs glued together on craft paper, except they have an unusual vibe that makes them not kids' work.

I carry some books with me to my bedroom and sprawl on the bed. I take the picture of Mom out of my knapsack and look at it. Does she have a picture of me she looks at sometimes? If she does, does she miss me? Does she wonder where I am, how I am?

I asked Gran once if Mom ever called her, or sent a letter, or got in touch in any way. Gran simply snorted. I couldn't tell if her snort meant, *don't be ridiculous, your mother'd never do that*, or if it meant if she ever did get in touch, Gran wouldn't tell her anything about me, or tell me about it.

I slip the picture back into the pocket of my knapsack and look at pictures of Sung dynasty ceramics and Japanese raku bowls until I guess I fall asleep.

Something wakes me up, and I see afternoon has passed into evening. Out the window the sky is that navy blue you get in the city from all the lights. It takes me a breath or two to remember where I am, and I lie there for another minute listening, trying to figure out what woke me up.

The bedroom door is open a crack—I learned not to shut it all the way near the end of when I was living at Gran's, when she was getting crazier, in case I needed an escape route. Tonight, light seeps in around the edges, thin and watery.

I get out of bed, open the door, and peek out. The hallway is empty. At the other end of the hall, the light in the kitchen glows. I hear the faint murmur of someone talking, the occasional crack of laughter. I pad down the hall as quietly as I can and stop just outside the kitchen door.

Francis is talking to someone. "I don't think so. Not much longer. . ."

I don't hear the rest because I turn and go back to my bedroom.

Quietly, I move the books onto the floor. Then I stretch out on the bed, trying to see if I can make sense of what I heard him say. As I try to find meaning, I start sinking into sleep, until a whisper of sound snaps me alert.

I open my eyes only a slit and see Francis ease the door further open. He comes into the room almost silently. I feel a twist of fear—have I been wrong about him all along? I lie completely still, barely breathing—but no, he goes over to the window and pulls the curtain closed. When he turns around, I see he has a blanket draped over his arm. He shakes it open and lets it float down lightly over me. Then he leaves, pulling the door behind him until only a splinter of light spills around its edge. I float there trying to figure out what's going on as the darkness rises around me, and I drift away on it.

~

By the time I get up the next morning, Francis has already left, but there's a note, "On the move tomorrow. Get your things packed. See you later."

I'm in the kitchen making coffee, wondering what to do on my last day in the city when it hits me like a truck—how could I be so dumb not to think of it earlier? Go check on Gran.

I won't visit her; that would be a disaster. Not that she'd call the cops or anyone. She doesn't trust them, but she might try to convince me to stay, might start pulling quotations out of the Bible and brandishing them like weapons. No, I won't go see her, but I'll check out the house, what kind of shape it's in, and then I'll leave.

It's a fifteen-minute streetcar ride west and a twenty-minute trek north. Walking along the leafy, tree-lined streets, I realize something I didn't understand when I lived here: Gran lives in a nice part of town—not the toniest by a long shot, but it's safe, fairly clean, "improving," as Francis would say. And I imagine the house prices are "improving" too.

It wasn't as desirable when she and my grandfather first moved here. My mother showed me photos once from when she was young. At the time, their neighbours were mostly working-class people, my mom said, a lot of them Portuguese, who built strong, solid houses with ceramic tiles set into the wall beside the front door showing the Immaculate Heart of Mary or the Bom Pastor. The modest front yards were surrounded by low brick walls; some of the walls had pieces of broken pottery embedded in them.

The original owners—the stonemasons, plumbers, electricians—have sold out and moved away, and the houses are being what Francis calls "gentrified." These days the electricians, plumbers, and stonemasons drive here from elsewhere to work on houses their parents or grandparents might have built and lived in. They park their vans on the streets and sidewalks, clogging traffic. There are the sounds of construction everywhere: hammering, drilling. A group of guys wearing hard hats stand around a driveway where fancy paving stones are being laid.

I stop three doors from Gran's, duck into the narrow alley that runs behind the houses on the street perpendicular to hers. I'm out of sight of anyone inside her place. It's the worst building on the block—on several blocks, in fact.

The roof is shot—the shingles crisped and curling up at the edges like the ones Francis pointed out at the farm near Shelburne. The whole place needs a paint job—the window frames, the front porch, the front steps. Weeds choke the front yard. The blinds are drawn; the house stares blankly at the street. I watch the place for five, maybe ten minutes, wondering if Gran will come out, stepping off smartly to do an errand, if I'll get a glimpse of her.

I think about how, when I lived there with her, Gran seemed so big, so powerful—like she told me, she fed and clothed me, she stood between me and the evil outside world. Now, standing at a distance, and with the distance I've travelled and the people I've met, I see she wasn't. She had power over me, yes. And part of her power was that she was the only family I had left. Dad was gone. Mom was gone. It felt like Gran was the only person I mattered to. She taught me other people were sinful and dangerous, school was bad, cops, teachers, everyone but her was a threat.

But that's not true. Sure, there's some bad stuff about Francis, but there are good things, too. The same with other people, there's a lot of good in people—Jean, the old lady we scammed, was sweet, she gave me cookies (not cookies I liked, but she didn't know, and she didn't have to give me any, it was generous of her). Ray seemed okay, as did Eddy.

So, when I think about Gran right now, what I see is someone who's scared, scared of the outside world, scared of anything being different from what she's used to. And because of her fear, she behaves in ways—she drove her daughter away, she drove me away—that leave her more and more alone in a world with less and less in it, a world shrinking around her.

Do I want to live in her world? I don't. I've seen outside of that world. Other worlds are possible than the one Gran lives in.

Did she love me? In her own way, I think. But that way is so shrunken and deformed—the way the world is warped when you look at it through old glass—it distorts everything she looks at, even the people she loves.

Maybe someday, I think—but then I ask myself: someday what? Do I want to see her? I don't, not right now. I don't trust her, and I don't trust me around her. Do I wonder if she's okay? I do, but not enough to knock on the door and talk to her.

After a while I take a deep breath, turn, and walk away.

8.

THE NEXT MORNING, IT'S STILL DARK out when Francis is rapping on my door. "Up and at 'em. Time to hit the road." In half an hour, we've packed up; my knapsack and his duffel bag are stashed in the space behind the front seat, he's fortified the wall between us, and we're heading east.

Traffic is already building, even this early, so it takes us a while to clear the city, and it's not until near Ajax he pulls off to eat.

Sitting across from each other in a strip mall diner, waiting for bacon and eggs, Francis says, "I've been doing some research, making enquiries. My intuition says, 'head east,' so east it is."

For someone in such a hurry to get going, once we're travelling, he seems to be in no rush. After breakfast, we head northeast. Over the next couple of weeks, we keep moving north and east through places with names I never knew before: Brooklin, Myrtle, Port Perry. We loop around Lake Scugog, dawdle in Lindsay. We hit rummage sales, antique markets, and yard sales picking up inventory or lightening it, depending on Francis's calculations.

There's Omemee, Peterborough. Francis seems relaxed and restless at the same time. We get out once in a while to wander around, get the flavour of each place, but we never stop for long. We pass through Trenton, Stirling, Tweed, then head south to Tamworth, Enterprise, Yarker, and land in Kingston.

It's Friday when we drive into town. He parks on a tiny side street—barely a street at all, only a block long, with maybe five houses on one side and a small park on the other—and wander downtown.

It's a brisk day, wispy clouds scudding across a sky the colour of a robin's egg. The light is so clear and sharp, it seems I can see each leaf shimmering on every tree. The shadows have crisp edges.

A block from Lake Ontario sits City Hall, with a massive copper dome. In front of it, on the side facing away from the lake, is an open square where vendors have set up their booths offering local produce, honey, bread, meat, flowers, crafts, clothing.

We walk around getting a feel for the place. Francis chats up a woman selling eggs and learns there's an antique market here on Sunday.

"So that's our weekend organized," he says to me.

We find a cheap motel on the edge of town, out past the military base. On Saturday, we familiarize ourselves with the square and the streets around it. Francis figures out where we'll park the truck, the various approaches to the market. As always, he figures out where we'll rendezvous, the escape routes if the situation goes south.

Sunday dawns warm and bright, the sun a blurry glow floating in the hazy sky.

Wasps are buzzing around trash cans at the edge of the square. Already it's humid, the air feels dense and sticky.

City Hall's dome towers above the rows of stalls that cover almost every square inch of the market square with all sorts of goods for sale, from blocky early Ontario furniture, to sports cards, to shiny Coca Cola signs nailed onto barn boards, to vintage clothing and memorabilia.

"They *call* it an antique market," Francis says, as we stand at the edge of the square, "because calling it *dead people's junk* would be a bad move. Collectibles is more accurate, though even that is stretching the truth a lot of the time." On overcast or rainy days, the items would look shoddy and cheap—"tatty," Francis calls them—but today, in the sunshine, they look shiny and appealing.

We get to the market around ten, when there's already a reasonable crowd. If we show up too early and there aren't enough other people around, we might stand out in vendors' memories, but as part of a crowd, we're just two faces among hundreds that all blur together.

The sellers lounge behind their tables, watching the crowds amble past: young urban professionals—as Francis derisively calls them—sipping their lattes; families with babies in buggies and toddlers racing around; older folks out for a stroll; collectors assessing the offerings.

I walk the perimeter while Francis wanders through the middle of the market. A minute or so after I've started my walk, a buzz starts up in my head, the hairs prickle on the back of my neck. I get the feeling I'm being watched, like that time before. I stop in front of a booth selling baseball cards and scan the crowd surreptitiously, but I can't see anyone with their eyes on me. Still, I can't shake the sensation, and when we rendezvous at the coffee shop he's chosen a couple of blocks away, I tell Francis about it.

He waves my concerns away. "Nothing to worry about. We'll be out of here in a couple of hours."

He points me in the direction of sterling silver grape scissors he saw at one booth, an onyx ring at another, and an Art Deco whiskey flask at a third. "All small," he says. "Pick them up and don't bother going back to the truck in between."

I'm surprised. This isn't standard operating procedure. Since when have we become so relaxed?

"It'll take you fifteen, twenty minutes at the most. Want to put money on it? Then we'll split this popsicle stand, on to richer pastures." He finishes his coffee and stands up. Discussion over.

I find the booth with the grape scissors, and palming them is easy. The onyx ring is more of a challenge because it's in a glass case, but I wait until the vendor is distracted by another customer—an older woman with bright orange hair and lots of chunky jewelry who wants to discuss a cocktail ring her mother gave her—to jimmy the lock on the case, the way Francis taught me, and swipe the ring.

The flask seems pretty straightforward, but I once again have the sense someone's watching me, so I turn away from the table and move on to a booth full of tchotchkes I would never pay attention to on any other day: wooden plaques with "Dance as if no one is watching, sing as if no one is listening" (bad advice, in my opinion), and variations on "Keep Calm and Carry On," most of them not very funny. I pick up a ceramic photo frame in the shape of a garland of kittens all tumbling together, and while I'm examining it, I scan the crowd around me, but nothing unusual catches my eye, so I move on to a pair of socks with "If you're up" printed on the right sole, and "Get me wine" on the left sole. Another quick check around me as I do this turns up nothing suspicious.

The coast clear, I put the socks down, wander away from that booth and circle back to the one with the flask.

I wait until the vendor selling the flask is deep in conversation with a customer before easing up to the table and sliding the flask into my jacket pocket—at which point a man's voice calls out loudly, "Hey, you—put that back." I freeze, hoping that if I stay still no one will notice me, I'll be able to drop the flask on the table and disappear, hoping whoever's shouting is yelling at someone else, not me.

"You—by the map table—put it back," the man yells again. This time it's clear it's me he's shouting at. A hush settles on the crowd. While I'm trying to decide what to do—slip the flask out of my pocket, confirming my guilt, or try to slip away—the vendor lunges sideways and grabs my wrist. He's a chunky middle-aged man, surprisingly quick for someone his size, with a fierce grip. I stare up into his red, angry face, only inches away from mine, and feel his hot breath.

Then a figure catches my eye. Behind the vendor, maybe six meters away, at the edge of the crowd on the far side of the market, stands Francis. He's staring at me, no expression on his face. I wait—for what? For him to come pushing through the crowd to save me? Yes—that's what I want. *Come save me, Francis,* I think, my breath shallow and fast.

He tips his head slightly, as if he's making a calculation, weighing risk and benefit. His eyes narrow, considering.

My heart races—it feels like it might explode, it's beating so hard.

I open my mouth to call out to him, but as I watch, he shakes his head almost imperceptibly.

And that's the instant I understand he's not going to save me: I'm expendable. If I tell anyone what's been going on, he'll deny it, all of it, deny knowing me, deny any involvement. I am on my own. He's cutting me loose.

My mouth clamps shut. I stand there paralyzed, all eyes on me, and watch as, leisurely, smoothly, he picks up a silver mint julep cup—the seller has turned to see what's going on. Francis raises the cup in my direction—an ironic toast—then slips it into his jacket pocket. He touches two fingers lightly to his forehead in a mock salute, turns, and saunters off without looking back.

19. Lost

9.

THE VENDOR HAS HIS FACE all up in mine, so close I can see the pores on his nose, the sheen of sweat on his forehead. "Drop it," he snarls. "Now!" He barks, when I'm not quick enough.

Suddenly, someone is beside me, a presence that seems to condense out of thin air. A woman, leaning forward, toward the vendor.

"I'm sorry," she says, her voice low, concerned. "Did my daughter—did she—?" I peek sideways, and watch as she widens her eyes at the guy on the other side of the table. She's not pretty, exactly, but pleasant-looking, a couple of inches taller than I am, slight, with dark hair cut short, and hazel eyes. Enough older than me so she does look like she could possibly be my mom—in her late thirties, is my guess. It only takes me a second to take all this in.

She rests her hand on my shoulder. "Hon," she says, her voice tinged with sadness and exasperation, "we've talked about this." Our eyes meet. Her gaze is intense; it's hard to read her expression. She turns back to the vendor. "She's been having a hard time since her Dad passed—" She pauses, the words fading out. She blinks a couple of times, then coughs, clears her throat and turns to me. "Hon, give the nice man back what you took." Surrounding us, a wall of faces, watching, some neutral, some curious, some frowning —all expectant, waiting.

I return her gaze, staring for a moment. Who is she? Why is she doing this? Why should I do what she tells me to do?

But Francis has disappeared, and a lot of people are watching us. It would be impossible for me to melt into the crowd and disappear right now. I'm trapped. I could try to deny I've done anything, but a quick calculation tells me that won't fly. I'm standing frozen, with my hand in my pocket. Her eyes meet mine. Her gaze hardens, she raises her eyebrows, the motion so subtle it's nearly invisible—*you're waiting, why?* If someone caught the look, they'd assume she's a mother losing patience with her uncooperative kid.

I pull the flask I lifted out of my pocket slowly, grudgingly, and place it in the middle of the table between me and the vendor. His hand darts forward and grabs it.

She holds my eyes a beat—*don't pull any funny stuff*—then leans towards the vendor and opens her purse. "How can I make this right?" she asks. She fishes out a wallet. "How much?" The guy shakes his head, waves away her offer. "It's okay," he says. "I don't want your money. As long as I have this—" he holds up the flask, "I'm good."

"Thank you," she says warmly, offering him an unsteady smile. There's a bright glimmer on her lower eyelid—the beginning of tears? She rests her hand lightly on his arm. "That's so kind of you." *Heartfelt words,* Francis would say in a knowing tone

"And I'm sorry for your loss," he adds.

She nods, as if it's too difficult to speak, grabs my arm, and leads me away, her grip tight, like Gran's was when she was on a tear.

People drift past, glancing at us. One woman says to her friend, "Wasn't that nice of him?"

"Poor woman," another lady mutters, looking sympathetically at my companion, then shooting me a glare.

The stranger is pulling me away from the booth. I resist, dragging my feet. I don't know who she is and I don't want to go anywhere with her. The only person I trusted even marginally was Francis, and he's gone, taken off, flown the coop, left me to deal with this on my own.

She stops and turns to face me, her hand still tight on my wrist. The grieving widow has disappeared. She pulls me close and leans in, her mouth beside my ear. Automatically I try to pull back, but I can't, she's stronger than me. Her voice is low and urgent, too quiet for anyone but me to hear. "You have two options: you can come with me, or I can walk you right back there and tell the man you stole the flask from that I'm not your mother. Then I'll take you to the two other booths you hit and you can hand back what you took from them. And then I'll figure out whether to call the cops. Your choice."

She holds up two fingers. "Two options." She holds up five fingers. "Five seconds. Because I want to find the man who dumped you, and he has a head start on us."

People walk past; their gazes skitter over us with curiosity.

I glare at her.

"Come on, hon," she says more loudly, in a sweet voice, tugging me towards the edge of the square. It occurs to me that when we get there, once the crowd has thinned, I could make a run for it, try to find Francis. Maybe it's all a mistake. He can't have made it far. I could try to get back to the truck and trailer—if I'm fast, I might get there when he does.

As if she's guessed what I'm thinking, she stops, her back to me. "He's gone," she says in a low, flat voice. "I watched him. I saw him look straight at you. I saw him turn and walk away. Very leisurely, very deliberate."

She turns and looks me straight in the eye. "If he was going to rescue you, he would have done it by now. You are on your own and I am your best option. By the way, there is no third option. I am not walking away from here and leaving you to your own devices. You come with me, or I take you to the police or Children's Services."

I feel a flash of anger. I don't know about her being the best option—the best option would be to find Francis and sort this all out—but I do know I don't see any other possibilities at this point. If Francis did want to get me out of this situation, he's had plenty of time to. I stop fighting.

"Okay. I'll go with you."

"Smart kid."

"Let go," I tell her. She gives me a measuring look then drops my hand. I whip my arm away and rub my wrist. It throbs a bit. She keeps walking across the square. I wait for a beat. Now she's let go of me, I could run off. But all I own is with Francis. He's gone, and lots of people saw what just happened—there's no place safe to hide here. It looks like she's right: my only choice is to go with her. I tell myself I can always take off later if I need to. I put my head down and tag along behind her.

As I follow, I look her over carefully. She's wearing jeans—not fashionable jeans, not famous brand name ones, but not mom jeans, either—a white t-shirt, and over it, an unbuttoned denim shirt. She's wearing the same type of all-purpose leather boots Francis wears, and has a lean build.

She walks—and I follow her—out of the market, onto a side street. She stops in front of an older blue Honda Civic that's seen better days. There's some rust around the wheel wells, a couple of scrapes and dents on the doors. It's a car that can fly under the radar the same way Francis's truck does.

She opens the passenger door, scoops a jumble of items off the seat—pamphlets and maps, by the looks of it—and tosses them into the back seat, which is buried under a blizzard of fast-food wrappers, paper fast-food bags, and coffee cups. "Get in," she says.

I know it's a bad idea to get in a car with—face it—a total stranger and go who knows where, but on the other hand, I don't see an alternative right now. She did save me from the angry vendor. For a moment a flicker of fear licks at me—I don't know who she is or what she's doing—but I have nowhere else to go, no one I can call. I decide to play along, at least for the moment.

Once we're in the car, she asks, "Where did you park?"

"What?"

"The truck and the trailer. Where did you park?"

How does she know about the truck and trailer? I decide there's no point in acting dumb.

"On the other side of City Hall, away from the lake."

"Give me directions."

"Left up here." As we drive, I wonder: do I even want to find Francis? I know how to look after myself now better than when I met him. I could get myself back to Toronto, find the kids I used to know. I've picked up some useful skills. Then I remember my knapsack, the picture of my mom.

He does not get to take that from me. I want it back.

But why does this woman want to find him? Is this a set-up? Is she a cop? Or maybe it's something worse—Francis has been in the game long enough to have pissed off a few people. Is she one of them, or working for one of them?

"Which way?" We're sitting at an intersection with a green light. I hesitate. "Every second we sit here, he gets farther away," she says.

"Go right."

By the time we get to where Francis parked, the truck and trailer are gone. I point at the empty space. "He's gone."

She looks over at me as if she's trying to decide whether I'm being straight with her. "Right," she says, as if she's reached a decision. Her mouth is set. She pulls a u-turn, drives back the way we came, and then takes the road over the causeway heading out of town.

It doesn't take me long to realize we're on our way to the motel where Francis and I were staying. How does she know? I glance sideways at her. She's driving fast but carefully, staring intently at the road, her chin tucked in.

"How—?" I start.

She looks over, then back at the road. She doesn't answer my question.

Which is when it occurs to me, I might be in the middle of an even bigger mess than I thought—maybe it's not simply me and Francis; it could be Francis is into something larger, more dangerous, and us moving "unassuming" objects was only a cover. This idea makes me nervous. She's going too fast for me to jump out of the car, but once we get to the motel—

"What are you going to do?" Her voice interrupts my thoughts. "Stand on the side of the road and hitchhike? Not the brightest idea."

I stare at her. But she's right, again.

"Kid," she says, "I get it that you don't want to go to the cops or Children's Services, right?"

"Yes. I mean, no—I don't." My voice sounds faint.

"Is there a responsible adult I can drop you off with? A mom or a dad?"

I think of Gran. "No."

"Then here's the deal, I want to find the guy who dumped you—for reasons of my own. Maybe you can help me, I don't know. You stick with me, and once we've tracked him down, we'll figure out what to do about you. It won't involve the cops or Children's Services. Okay?"

The motel's up the hill, about half a kilometer further on. I haven't heard any better offers, and I always have the option of bailing if I need to.

I take a deep breath. "Okay."

~

When we get to the motel, the only vehicle in the parking lot is the dinged-up red Ford, which has been sitting there the whole time Francis and I have been here, the one that looks like it died in the parking lot and has been left there to disintegrate. No sign of Francis, the truck, or the trailer.

The woman lets out a breath of irritation and slaps the steering wheel. "Any idea where he might have gone?"

I shake my head. "He just said we were going east."

She leans forward, crosses her hands on top of the steering wheel, and rests her forehead on her wrists. After a few seconds, she straightens, puts the car into reverse, turns around in the motel parking lot, and pulls onto the road.

10.

"MY NAME'S DERYN," SHE SAYS. We're speeding away from the city, through countryside.

"Darren?" I repeat. "I thought that was a guy's name."

She shakes her head. "Deryn. D-e-r-y-n. It means *bird* in Welsh."

I glance at her, then away. How much to tell her? Like Francis taught me, knowledge is power. Like Francis also said, don't give information to strangers. "I'm Frankie."

She eyes me, shrugs, then turns back to the road. "Sure. If you say so."

"No, it's—"

"It's fine," she interrupts, waving a hand dismissively. "If you don't want to tell me the truth you don't have to. You don't owe me anything."

The only sound for a while is the road humming under the car's wheels. Then she says, "What I do want to know is what you were up to with him—"

I open my mouth, start to deny—she shoots me a long, cool look. "You can skip that part. I've had my eye on you two since Enterprise, three days ago."

It's a kick in the gut to know she's been watching us for so long and neither one of us noticed, but then I remember times

I sensed someone was following me, the moments I thought I was being observed, the way the hair prickled on the back of my neck. I told Francis, but he brushed it off. I was right after all. Knowing this doesn't make me feel any better.

"Your move at the market today—palming the flask—it was a pro move. Smoothly done. If someone hadn't had their eye on you, they wouldn't have noticed. Is he your father, the man you were working with?" I steal a glimpse of her again, then I stare out the window.

"No," I say, a little too loudly, a little too defensively.

"Okay," she says. "A friend then. Although most *real* friends don't drag their buddies into illegal activities. A lesson I learned the hard way."

While she talks, I'm thinking—so that's how she knew where we were staying. And if she's been watching us that long, what else does she know? What's she going to do with what she knows? What's she going to do with me?

"We weren't really hurting anyone," I say.

"I suppose it depends on your definition of hurt," she says, slouching in her seat, appearing to relax slightly. "You probably didn't put anyone's life in danger, I grant you that, but you don't know how badly those people may need the money they get from selling those things."

I open my mouth to argue, but it's so close to what I know is true I shut it again.

"I've spent a lot of time in these grey areas," she continues. "I can argue both sides of a question, but I do know which side is right."

"I figured if I left the best items and took only the cheaper ones, I'd be helping them," I tell her. "Cutting their losses." I stare at my hands.

"That might help you feel less guilty," she says, "about stealing."

"I know it's stealing," I say. "But—"

"But?" she says. There's an odd expression on her face—amusement? "It's complicated, is that it?" It sounds like she's teasing me.

"No," I say, feeling unhappy. "It's stealing. It always has been."

"So, what are you going to do about it?"

"Stop stealing."

"What about him?"

It sounds like an accusation. I want her to understand about Francis, that what we were doing was bad, but he wasn't bad, or at least not all bad, not to me, most of the time. . .until about half an hour ago.

"He took care of me," I say. Then I shut down because she's right, it is complicated, and I don't feel like trying to explain it all right now.

She asks more questions, but I just give mumbled answers. I stare at the landscape speeding past, trying to figure out what to do. *What would Francis do?* I ask myself. But then I realize, Francis would probably never end up in this situation. I can't imagine anyone grabbing him by the wrist and dragging him anywhere.

Suddenly Deryn's talking again. "So, Frankie."

"Yes?"

"As long as you're with me, no stealing, okay? You steal, I hand you over to the authorities. Is that clear?"

"Yes."

She stares at me, raises her eyebrows.

"I get it," I say. "No stealing."

She reaches over and turns on the radio. Some jangly, rock-y music flows into the car. She pulls onto the main highway out of town and I see we're heading west. I wonder where we're going. I've decided that in this situation Francis would keep his mouth shut and his eyes open. He'd be on the look-out for opportunities, but he'd also be coming up with an exit plan.

After a while Deryn says, "I need to eat. What about you?"

I'm starving. Francis and I had an early start this morning—the plan was to grab a meal after the market, now *this* is after the market. "Yeah, I'm hungry," I tell her.

"Okay. We can't take long. You can use the washroom if you need to."

We pull off at the next rest stop. She buys a couple of plastic-wrapped sandwiches, some yogurts, and drinks.

Then we're back in the car pulling onto the highway.

"Can you unwrap a sandwich for me, please?" she asks. I peel the plastic wrap off one and hand it to her. "Thanks." She takes a bite.

"Any of this look familiar?" she asks, waving the sandwich at the scenery out the car window.

"Nope. I don't remember coming this way with him."

"What do you remember?"

I describe the beginning, how he found me on the street. I explain how, early on, I was paying such close attention to what he wanted me to learn, it took me a while to put together what was going on. How stuff became all mixed up, the cities and towns blurring together, but as time went on, they gradually became distinct from one another.

We ride in silence for a while, then she says, "I understand you might not trust me. If I were in your shoes, I wouldn't trust me." She waves her hand at the plastic bag with food in it. "Eat, eat," she says. "And while you're at it, can you pop one of those drinks open for me?"

I open one and hand it to her, then unwrap a sandwich for me. She knocks back some of the drink, then says, "A couple of questions—so it's all clear to me." She glances at me. "Do you have a home to go to?"

Thinking of Gran, I look at her, then away.

"Is that a 'no,' or a 'yes, but I don't want to go back there'?'"

I stay silent. I'm not sure I want to tell her.

"I mean," she continues, "your choices seem to me to be Children's Services, or wherever you came from before. . . him. What's his name, by the way?"

"Francis."

"Seriously?" she says.

I shrug. "It's what he told me."

"And you're Frankie." She lets the words hang in the air for a moment, then she sips her drink again. "So, as I was saying, Children's Services? Or. . .?" she falls silent.

Before I realize it, I've spoken into the silence. "My gran's."

"No mother?" Her eyebrows go up. "No father?"

I shake my head. "Only my gran."

"Tell me about your gran," she says. "Since it doesn't seem like you're in much of a hurry to get back to her."

"I know she thinks she's doing what's right—"The words pop out. I clamp my mouth shut.

"But. . ." she prompts.

"Well, she always keeps the house so cold."

"Wear more clothes."

"And the dented cans of food."

Bit by bit, I tell her about Gran, the rules, the prayers, no TV, no cell phone. Only the bare minimum, so Deryn understands why I don't want to go back there, but not enough information that she could track Gran down somehow. She listens in silence.

When I finish, she says, "Yup. Doesn't sound like much fun at your gran's."

I think about this. "But I'd rather go to Gran's than to Children's Services."

She considers. "Is that what you want? Because I can take you to your gran's."

"What I really want," I tell her, "is to find him—find Francis." The words come out in a rush. I want my knapsack back; I want the photo of my mom. I'm not going to tell her that—I don't trust her; if she gets her hands on it, she might use it to get me to do things to get it back—but what I want is the photo. "I want to ask him why he dumped me. I thought we were partners. Friends. He said we were." Which is partly true. Like Francis said, the closer you can stick to the truth, the more genuine what you say sounds.

"You think that's a good idea?"

"I don't care about good ideas," I snap. The question bugs me. What do good ideas have to do with this? I want to understand what happened and why.

"Whatever he did he might do again," she points out, "charm you, play you."

"He didn't charm me," I say. I start to add, "he didn't play me," but maybe I'm wrong, maybe he did, at least to some extent. He managed it so I did what he wanted me to, one way or another. I think about this for a second. "He took care of me," I continue. "He taught me a lot—about artifacts, and other things. We were tight, a team—he said so. That's why I don't understand..." The words trail off.

"You know," she says, "you go looking for something, you don't always get the answers you're hoping for. You may think there's an answer, but..."

I turn to look out the window again. The sky is wide and empty, a speckless blue.

"He has something I want," I tell her.

She looks at me quizzically but doesn't say anything.

~

After about an hour we take the turn-off at a town called Belleville. We pass a mall, drive down a wide street with the same mixed bag of restaurants, fast food places, strip malls, bars, and other miscellaneous shops I've seen in a lot of the places Francis and I have passed through, the new buildings surrounding the older downtown core.

Deryn seems to have a destination in mind: we pass a grey stone church with a tall, pointy spire, a library in a newer building, and then we're at a covered market with booths in neat, tidy rows.

She drives past it and parks a couple of blocks away. Then she leans over, reaches into the glove compartment, fishes around in it, and pulls out two pairs of sunglasses, puts on a pair and hands me the other. When we get out of the car, she says, "Hold on." She pops the trunk, pulls out two blue baseball caps and hands me one. "Not much of a disguise, but better than nothing."

Why is she carrying around disguises? That's peculiar. Something to think about. I put on the hat and sunglasses.

"So," she says, "we'll each do a once-around—" the phrase snags in my ear. I thought it was a term only Francis and I used. Maybe other people use it, too? "And we'll rendezvous." She stands beside me, surveying the market. "Fifteen minutes? You think you'll have enough time?"

Enough time for what? The place doesn't seem too crowded. "I guess." What does she want me to do?

"We're looking for Francis. If you see him, give him space. You spook him, he'll take off. Do you have a phone?" I shake my head.

"Hunh. Well, we'll have to sort that out later. It'd be a lot easier if you did. If you see him—I know—take off your cap and scratch the back of your head, okay? I'll be keeping an eye on you. If you take off your cap, I'll make a beeline to you, understand?"

"Yup." I say, although I'm thinking maybe I won't. If I see Francis, I'll get up close to him, tell him I want to know what's going on and that if he doesn't tell me, I'll make a scene.

Deryn pats my shoulder and walks away. It's odd, the pat, absent-minded, the casual, familiar kind of thing you do to an old friend or someone you're really comfortable with, as if we've known each other a long time.

I watch her for a second, then turn and walk in the opposite direction.

The humid morning has turned into a muggy day. Everyone's moving slowly. Some people are fanning themselves with their hats, patting their faces and necks with handkerchiefs or bandanas, others pluck at their shirts, which are sticking to them in the heat.

Why here, I wonder. What made Deryn decide to come here? I don't remember ever being in this place with Francis. What does she know about him? She seems to be familiar with the game without me telling her—the "once-around" comment—what else does she know about it and him? I walk up to a booth selling vintage comic books wrapped in clear plastic. I pull one out of the display box they're filed in. It's an old Batman comic. The vendor—a skinny older dude with a neatly-trimmed beard, who's wearing a fringed leather vest covered in beaded rose designs—hurries over. He plucks the comic out of my hands, and files it carefully back in the box.

"These are collector's items," he says in a high, tight, clear voice. "They are not for you to read."

All right, I think. I'm tempted to try and lift one while he's not looking simply because he's so obnoxious, but I don't want to draw attention to myself, so I move on. Beside him is a booth selling semi-precious stones, which I'm somewhat curious about but not enough to linger, and next is a vendor selling plaques with inspirational sayings like, "Follow your dreams—they know the way," which doesn't even make sense. Then someone moving off to my left catches my eye.

I can only see the back of the person's head. I watch him briefly, then look away. I don't want whoever it is to get the feeling someone's watching them. It's a man, by the looks of it, tall, rangy, and moving the way Francis moves: a loping walk with a tiny bounce of anticipation in it. He's wearing jeans and a white shirt, which was what Francis was wearing earlier under his old leather jacket.

I start ambling after the person, always keeping at least a couple of people between us, stopping when he stops, turning away to check out whatever booth is in front of me so he can't get a look at my face.

I scan my surroundings. Deryn's nowhere to be seen. She may be watching and I can't see her, so I keep following the person who may be Francis as he makes his way across the market, past booths, to the other side of the plaza.

I'm aiming for inconspicuous as I follow him, but by the time I get to the edge of the market, where I last noticed him, he's disappeared. I stand staring in the direction the person went, toward a car park jammed with cars, vans, and pick-ups, but there's no Francis, there's no one resembling him anywhere in sight, no truck and trailer like his visible.

Abruptly, Deryn's beside me. "Did you see him?" She's surveying the parking lot.

"I don't know. I didn't get a close look at his face. The way he moved looked like Francis, but by the time I got here, he was gone."

"Come on," she says, her hand on my shoulder, turning me and steering me back the way we came. "If it was him, we're on the right track, but we won't know for a while, if ever. If it wasn't him, well, either way, we should get moving." She doesn't sound angry. Maybe she didn't get that I was planning to take off.

"Okay," I say.

11.

WHEN WE GET BACK TO THE CAR I take off the cap and toss it onto the dashboard, open the glove compartment and shove the glasses in. Deryn starts the car and pulls out into traffic. I figure we're going back to the highway, but she takes us in another direction, along city streets running parallel to the waterfront.

As the city drops away behind us, she reaches over to turn on the radio.

Before she can, I say, "You started watching us in Enterprise."

She pulls her hand away from the on/off knob. "Yup."

"Why?"

"You caught my eye, the two of you. I was curious."

"How did we catch your eye?"

She shrugs. "I've had jobs that taught me how to pay attention. I saw you at the flea market there and I could tell you were working really hard to fly under the radar."

"You could tell?"

"Mm-hm." She nods. "I doubt most people would have noticed—you're both pretty adept. But it was how you tried not to be noticed that I noticed." She starts to say more, then pauses. After a beat she continues. "There are things normal people do that you didn't."

"Like what?"

She gives me a look, grins, shakes her head. Not going to give away what Francis calls *trade secrets.*

"You saw what we were doing?"

"Yup."

"And you didn't call the cops?"

She waves a hand dismissively. "Like you said, you weren't doing much damage. Not in the big scheme of things. And I knew if the police became involved it would complicate the situation." She's answered my questions in a manner of speaking, but as with Francis, I have the feeling I'm not getting the whole story. What was she doing when we "caught her eye"? Just hanging around? Who just hangs around flea markets watching people? A cop? Security?

"What jobs have you had that taught you to pay attention?"

"Well. . ." She lets the word peter out. For a few seconds we ride in a silence that feels charged with—irritation? Exasperation? Then she laughs and the tension breaks. "Fair enough, Frankie," she says. "You've told me a lot about you. Here's what I'll tell you about me. I know the antiques business, *the game*, as you called it. I was introduced to it by. . .someone close to me. I did it for a while. I'm not in it anymore. I'm not a cop. I don't work for the cops, although I have passed them information sometimes. Let's see—" she rubs the back of her neck "—I was married once but I'm single now. I've had a few different lives. In one of them I was a private investigator, a detective."

So that explains the baseball caps, the sunglasses—cheap, easy disguises. "A detective?" I repeat. "How did you become a detective?"

"I fell into it, more or less. A friend was doing it and recommended me. I had certain skills. The guy who owned the company decided to take me on. He said I seemed to be someone who could keep my eyes open and my mouth shut." She throws me a look.

"Oh, yeah? What was it like, being a detective?" I ask, ignoring the implication in her glance. "Sounds interesting."

"Everyone thinks it sounds interesting, but it usually wasn't. It mostly involved doing surveillance for insurance companies. Like, watching to see if the guy who's filed a disability claim due to back problems he says were caused by a fall at work is the same guy who's hauling stacks of shingles up a twenty-foot ladder to fix his roof—those types of situations. But I picked up some useful skills."

After a while I ask, "What were your other lives?"

She seems to consider the question before answering, then she says, "I worked in, uh..." she pauses, searching for the right word, "a re-sale situation—finding items and connecting them with a buyer—then for a while I was a journalist, I did some ghostwriting, and some photography."

"Which was best?"

She considers this. "I think I liked journalism. Certainly more than doing surveillance. Okay? Do you have enough information?"

It's interesting, I think, how cold, hard facts can tell you almost nothing about a person. "I guess it'll have to do," I say.

She raises her eyebrows, amused. "I guess it will." Whatever it was, irritation or exasperation, seems to have passed.

Overhead, big, puffy clouds sail slowly through the clear blue sky. A question occurs to me. "When you were my age..." I say, and let the sentence hang there.

She looks at me, waiting for me to finish. We pass a modest gas station/convenience store. Out front, beside the entrance, a vending machine catches my eye; the sign on it says: "Worms for sale."

"When I was your age," she prompts.

"Yeah—what were you doing when you were my age?"

"When I was your age," she says slowly, "my family broke. Or maybe it was a while before that."

Broke. I know about families breaking. I know how my family broke: Dad took off and left Mom and me on our own, then Mom went away and left me with Gran. It all happened when I was really young, so mostly what I remember is my time with Gran and, to me, that was how life was. When Mom was around, well, I have some memories of that time. When it was only Gran and me, I missed the way it had been when Mom was in the picture, but I also knew I'd been really young then, and my recollections of the time were fuzzy, my memories of Mom felt more like dreams than real. And living with Gran never felt like what I remembered family feeling like when I was with Mom.

Gran and me felt like how Francis described an old breakfront we saw once that had obviously been mended over time by a whole bunch of different people—"cobbled together." We didn't feel like a real family. I'd see other families—moms, dads, kids—doing stuff, looking like they were having fun (not always, not all of them), and they seemed to be *together* in a way Gran and I weren't. They were all inside a bubble that made them a group; they were all on the same team. I wanted to be inside a bubble the way they were, safe with other people, to be a part of a family like the ones I saw, to be on a team. Instead, I was on the outside looking in. It was like they had knowledge I didn't—how to be a family—and I didn't know how to learn it.

"How?" I ask. "How'd it break?"

She shakes her head. "We'd been a family, and then we weren't. We'd been together, and then we fell apart. Whatever it was that had held us together stopped holding us together."

"How did you feel?" The question pops out before I really know I've asked it. Maybe it will make her angry, talking about this.

"Like it was my fault, of course," she says. "Kids always think that. If I'd been better, if I'd been—I don't know—if, if, if. It should have been me, not—" she stops bites down on what she was about to say, shakes her head "—maybe what happened wouldn't have happened. Maybe we'd still be a happy family. And if it hadn't happened, how would my life be different?"

It's a surprise to hear a grown-up say this—she felt like what happened was her fault. I've felt the same way, like it must have been something I did that made Dad leave—was I a bad baby, did I cry a lot? Maybe if I'd been a better kid, if I'd behaved better, Mom would have stuck around. And it didn't help to have Gran telling me I was sinful and bad—it confirmed to me what had happened was my fault. And I wondered, too, if Dad hadn't left, would he and Mom and me have been a tight, happy family like the ones I used to see? And if he hadn't left, Mom and I wouldn't have ended up at Gran's, and Mom wouldn't have left, and maybe I wouldn't have run away, and on and on and on.

"It took me a long time to figure out," Deryn continues, "and it's not really obvious—a thing can break in your life, but it doesn't have to break you. It might break you," she adds, "and that's tough. But it might not. It might damage you, but then you look at the situation and think, 'what have I learned?' And if you can learn from what happened, then you start to have tools for navigating life."

"Francis said something once—what doesn't damage you makes you stronger. Like that, you mean?"

"Not so sure about that." She shakes her head, her mouth tight. "There's damage, for sure. Then there's collateral damage."

~

The next town is Trenton. Deryn checks the clock on the dashboard. "We'll have a look around," she tells me. "Keep your eyes open for garage sales, flea markets, rummage sales." Then she says, "Keep moving or spend the night?" It sounds like a question she's asking herself, not me. "Port Hope'll be the next stop."

We drive around for about half an hour, but the place seems sleepy, not much going on, and after about twenty minutes, we're back on the highway heading west.

We get to Port Hope about forty-five minutes later. For supper we go out for burgers, then she signs us into a motel. It's nicer than the ones Francis and I stayed at. We leave the front desk, and she walks to the car to grab her bag from the trunk. She's about to slam the trunk shut when she focuses on me, almost as if she's noticing me for the first time. "You're going to need some clothes," she says. "We'll have to get you some tomorrow."

Once we're inside, she drops her bag on the bed closest to the bathroom.

"Okay, let's do some digging." I don't know what she means until she opens her bag, pulls out a laptop, sets it on the bed, and turns it on. She keys in the motel's wifi password.

"So, you want to find Francis?" she says.

I'm lying on the other bed. "Yeah."

"All right," she says. "Lucky for you I have some free time right now, and I know a thing or two about finding lost people and people who don't want to be found. Tell me what you know about him. Every piece of information, every detail you can remember, no matter how unimportant it might seem to you."

This makes sense. I start to think about it, and I realize: what do I really know about Francis? Not much, it turns out. "It's odd," I say, "we spent a lot of time together, all day every day for a long time, but—"

I tell her about Phoebe. I tell her the story he told me about running away to join the circus, how his leg was injured, how he became involved in what he calls the "antiques" business.

"I don't know where he came from," I say. "I don't even know if Francis is his right name."

"What do you think?"

"Could be," I say, shrugging. "But maybe not."

"What was he like? What kind of person was he?"

"He was okay. There was no funny stuff, no sexual stuff." I explain how he built a wall of books, the toolbox, bag lunches, and pamphlets between us on the truck seat, how we didn't share a room for a long time. I tell her what he said about Gran and her demons, how it sounded like he understood her, how he didn't make fun of her, which was part of why I began to think he might be all right.

"Come here." She pats the bed beside her. "Pay attention. We're going to do some research." I sit beside her and watch her type *Francis Person* into the keyword search bar. This brings up a choice of a whole bunch of personal trainer websites, so she narrows the search, and articles about one of the popes come up. She noodles around online for a while longer but has no success finding any information about the Francis we're looking for.

She has better luck when she searches Phoebe Person, but none of the people who pop up fit what we know about Francis's Phoebe, and they're mostly way older than his daughter would be. There's an obituary for a Phoebe Person, but it's from 1901—"long before even Francis was a gleam in his parents' eyes," Deryn says.

After this she shuts down her computer, finds the TV remote, and passes it to me.

While I'm watching a show about a bunch of people who seem to spend all their time in a coffee shop, Deryn pulls pyjamas out of her bag, goes into the bathroom, and comes back out wearing them. She climbs into bed and pulls the blanket up to her chin. Lying on her back, gazing up at the ceiling, she asks, "Any guesses where he might go?"

I consider this for a moment, my eyes still on the TV. "He never told me where we were going. Like I said, this last time all he said was we were heading east."

She punches her pillow and turns on her side.

At the end of the episode, I turn off the TV and shut off the light. The details of the room disappear, flattened out by the blackness. I stare at the ceiling, trying to figure out where Francis might be. He said we'd be travelling east. But maybe he just brought me to Kingston to dump me, and now he's headed back the way we came. Or maybe he's on his way to Montreal, or points further east—those people he's mentioned in the Maritimes.

I listen to Deryn's breathing, slow and steady. Every now and then the lights of a car going past on the highway track across the walls, and the hard edges of the world spring into sharp relief. Then the car passes, the lights disappear, the shadows flood back like ink spreading in water, and eventually they swallow me into sleep.

~

The next morning, I wake up before Deryn. There's an armchair beside my bed, between the bed and the window, and I'm sitting in it when she rolls onto her back and opens her eyes. She lies there for a minute, quiet. Then her gaze hops around the room until it lands on me and stops. When she first sees me, she frowns for an instant, like she's not sure who I am, and then a careful, blank expression slides into place. She rolls over, sits up, leans forward, and rubs her eyes, then she straightens and stretches, arching her back.

She drops her arms and lets out her breath. "Right," she says abruptly, as if she's reached a decision. She disappears into the bathroom, and I hear the sound of the shower running. A few minutes later she steps out, dressed in jeans and a t-shirt toweling her hair dry. "So," she says, "breakfast, and then we have to get you some clothes—before you get too stinky." She wrinkles her nose at me.

It's puzzling, how sometimes she's tough and other times she's playful, like now. It puts me off balance. I can't tell if she likes me, or if she's keeping me around because I'm useful. How could I be useful to her? I've told her all I know about Francis, which turns out to be not much.

We eat at a greasy spoon, like one Francis would choose, then she takes me to a store and buys me two pairs of new jeans, three new t-shirts (no words or pictures on them, I tell her), socks, and underwear. I put on some of the new clothes. They feel crisp and fresh. She asks the saleswoman for an extra shopping bag and drops my old clothes in it, and we get back in the car.

Then, because it's bugging me—and what do I have to lose?—I ask her, "Why are you doing all this? You rescued me at the market, you're feeding me, you're buying me clothes. Why?"

For a moment she's quiet, then she tells me, "Let's say I recognize the juncture where you find yourself. I was once in a similar situation. It wasn't exactly congruent, but it was similar."

"And you want to help?"

She purses her lips. "Motives are rarely so transparent. But that's part of it."

It's a half-answer—a response Francis might give—but the fact she admits helping is only part of why she's doing it, makes me think she's being honest, not painting herself as a guardian angel swooping in to save me. I'd like to know what the rest of her reasons for helping me are, but I keep my mouth shut. If she can help me find Francis, that's all I need.

12.

"LET'S GET SOME SNACKS to take on the road."

We find a grocery store in a mall, in a big, bright building with wide aisles and eye-catching displays. Gran always did the shopping. I'd go along to help carry the groceries, but she chose the store and the food. She always went to this old, dark store, with crowded aisles and chipped linoleum on the floor, because the people who owned it were part of her church and they'd sell her dented cans and cans missing their labels for cheap. Here, the shelves are stocked with all sorts of odd food and food-adjacent creations I've seen before but have never tried: whipped marshmallow topping, jam and peanut butter mixed together in a jar.

"My gran would *never* let me have this," I tell Deryn, pulling the jar off the shelf to check it out.

"You really have led a sheltered life, haven't you?" Deryn says. She takes the jar from me and tosses it into the shopping cart.

"How old are you, anyway?" she asks off-handedly. She's comparing two loaves of bread, one in each hand.

Why does she want to know? I debate telling her the truth. The less she knows about me the better, but then there's her long, cool gaze, the way she looks at me, skeptical, with the suggestion of impatience. What would I gain by lying? What would be lost by telling the truth? "Fifteen," I say.

"Hmm," she says thoughtfully. "A bit old to be learning about Goober."

We drive around Port Hope, which is a pretty town. "Too early in the week for the Farmer's Market," she says. "And probably no garage sales on the go. Maybe we can find a flea market, although it's unlikely. Let's take a look."

As she predicted, there are no garage sales or flea markets to be found, and the one antique store we stumble across is closed until later in the week. "Right," she says. "Let's get coffees, and we're out of here."

Once we're on the highway she says, "I want you to try and remember the towns and markets you know for certain the two of you visited."

It's hard for me to figure out where we went at the beginning. I was busy learning the game and rarely looked up to see where we were.

"That was probably to his advantage," she points out. "If you hadn't worked out at that early stage and he'd had to get rid of you, he wouldn't have wanted you to know his route."

We come to the conclusion that very early on, Francis and I were probably in the Kitchener/Waterloo/Guelph area, because I have a memory of black horse-drawn carriages rolling slowly along the side of the road as cars sped past.

Later, we were at a place in eastern Ontario I thought was called Meritville. "Merrickville, likely," Deryn says. She describes it to me—old stone buildings on a river—and it sounds like it might be the place.

Bit by bit we piece together a rough map of my travels with him, moving west from Toronto at first, keeping to small towns most of the time, skirting the larger centres, swinging north, then looping south and further west, turning back east, going north again, then south to pass through Toronto. And after that, traveling north and east and ending up in Kingston, where Francis cut me loose.

There's at least one place we seem to have visited a couple of times, the town with a mill where he met the woman at a restaurant and where later we stopped at that antique store. There may have been other places we passed through more than once, but that's the only one that stands out in my memory. As with a lot of things about Francis, the specifics of our travels are vague and uncertain.

"I've changed my mind," Deryn announces, pulling off the highway. She drives to a coffee place, gets her laptop, and we go inside. We order coffees and sandwiches and settle at a table near the window.

Deryn types in the names of every place we figure Francis and I visited. What we find are newspaper articles mostly about the history of each town or market, nothing more dramatic. Then we check auction house websites, estate sales. It becomes clear that during the time Francis and I were together, he organized it so he left no trace: he had a cell phone, but I never saw him online. He seemed to do all his trading face to face, and all the transactions I saw were in cash, so what trail would he leave? Which was the point, of course. But we keep searching. I'm not sure exactly what we're looking for, but maybe I'll know it when I see it.

Every once in a while, as we're researching the towns he and I may have visited, it seems like we catch a fleeting glimpse of him—a shadow moving at the edge of our vision.

"Oh," she says, animated, "we may be on the right track. Listen to this." It's a police report from Clarington—"Just up the road from here," she tells me—an incident from yesterday. "'Widower Jerome Gopper called police to report a Royal Worcester ceramic figurine missing, perhaps stolen," she reads. "'It was a fortieth wedding anniversary gift from my late wife,' Mr. Gopper reported, 'a cock-redstart on gorse. I'm a birdwatcher, you see. I can't imagine who would take it.'

"According to police, there was no sign of a break-in. Asked if there had been any unusual activity in the area recently, Mr. Gopper replied, 'No, nothing to speak of. It's a quiet community. Although there was a fellow knocked on my door the other day whose truck broke down and he had to make a phone call. . .'"

I imagine Francis—if it was him—walking back to the pickup, pulling the figurine out from under his jacket, cradling it carefully as he inspected it, climbing into the truck, setting it gingerly on the seat beside him, and driving off. But Francis is expert at what he does, and careful, so he seems to move around nearly invisibly.

That glimpse—and it may not even have been him—is the only one we find. There's nothing else, silence. If it was him, he has evaporated, disappeared.

13.

THEN SOMETHING OCCURS TO ME. Or *someone* occurs to me: Eddy.

"I have an idea," I tell Deryn.

"Spill," she says. She listens as I tell her in more detail about Eddy, about us going there, about Francis horse-trading with him.

"Eddy might know how to get in touch with him," I tell her. Why didn't I think of this before?

"Try and remember everything you can about Eddy. If we can find him, he might lead us to Francis."

This makes sense. I close my eyes and try to visualize the day we visited Eddy. I describe the trip to Toronto. It was hot. I tell her how it felt in the truck, close and fuggy; even with the windows rolled down the warm, humid air flowed into the truck and felt almost as thick and sticky as syrup. I was stiff, because I'd been sitting around for so long that day. "I was itchy, cranky."

The closer we got to Toronto, the wider and busier the highway grew. There were streetlights towering overhead, clusters of brilliance against the dark night sky. They whipped past as we sped along—there was a rhythm to them. I tell her how we picked up dinner, Indian food.

How Francis turned off the highway onto narrower, darker

streets, and slowed down. The tall lights were gone, we were in the dark, the streets mostly empty as we moved through a wasteland of industrial parks. And then there was a grey blocky concrete warehouse-type building with a flashing neon sign high in one corner, a spot of bright colour in the darkness, out of place in all the gloom, words flickering on and off: "Lougheed's Haulage," I tell her.

She keys the name into her computer and links appear on the left side of the screen; on the right side is a photograph of a square grey building with a neon sign. Beneath the photo is a Toronto address. "Is this it?"

"Looks like it."

We stare at the screen. "Do you think you could find your way to Eddy's from there?"

"Pretty sure."

"Okay, we'll give it a try." She plugs Lougheed's address into her phone. "Right. Let's go."

We take what's left of the coffee and sandwiches back to the car, and she pulls onto the highway.

The trip to Toronto takes about an hour. From Lougheed's, it's not too hard for me to figure out the way to Eddy's. We continue along the road to a T-intersection where I try to remember which way we turned that night. I decide we should go left. Deryn says if we don't find the place in ten minutes, no big deal, we'll backtrack and go the other way, but not much later I see Eddy's. "There it is," I say, pointing at the derelict-looking warehouse in the middle of the nearly empty lot.

It's still the same: the ground floor windows still boarded up, the same graffiti on the walls, the same rusting car sitting right where it was the night Francis and I dropped in. Today, I realize Eddy probably keeps it this way on purpose. It works for him to have the place look run-down: *nothing of interest going on here.*

Deryn drives about half a block past Eddy's and parks on the shoulder of the road.

"What do you think?" she asks. "Will Eddy be weirded out if you turn up with a stranger in tow, asking questions?"

I stare at the building, replaying that night in my memory. "He was kind to me," I tell her. "He gave me a blanket and pillow; he made me breakfast."

"Did he seem like the type of guy to freak out if strangers—well, one stranger—showed up on his doorstep?"

I think about this. "No." I shake my head. I think Eddy would be cool. He seemed careful and cautious—guarded—a guy who could handle most situations. A guy to have a back-up plan. Or two. "I think he'd be okay"

"All right," she says. "We'll go with your gut."

We climb out and walk up the road and across the lot to the warehouse. She tells me to stand where I can be seen by whoever's inside the building, and then she bangs on the door beside the loading dock Francis and I drove up to. When nothing happens after a few minutes, she picks up a rock and hammers on the door again. Dents in the door suggest she probably isn't the first person to come up with this solution. Still no answer. She steps back and throws the rock at the upstairs window where I told her the kitchen area is. A face flashes into view, then disappears. A couple of minutes later the door swings open.

It's Eddy. To someone else, he might seem a bit intimidating, his tats, his quiet intensity; to me he feels familiar, almost like a friend. First, he examines Deryn, frowning, then he glances over at me. I swear he does a double-take; his eyes widen in recognition then move past me as he examines the lot behind me, the street. He frowns. "Where's, uh—?" he asks, his voice the way I remember it, low, even, and quiet.

I shake my head. "He's not here. It's me. And her, Tara."

Deryn said not to use her real name. After my time with Francis, this made sense. We decided on Tara because it sounds similar to Deryn in case I slip.

"Tara," he repeats, peering at her more closely.

"Eddy, I need your help," I tell him.

He turns back to me, his face carefully neutral, stares at me for a second. He reaches a decision, jerks his head at the warehouse behind him. "Come on in."

I step past him, through the doorway. Deryn follows. Behind us, Eddy leans out, gives the area around the warehouse a quick once-over, then steps inside, pulls the door shut, and stands there staring at us. "Where's Francis?"

"That's the help I need."

"Hunh," he says, staring at me. It's a short sound, like a cough. He looks Deryn over again, seems to weigh some considerations.

"Okay," he says after a moment. "Let's go." He crosses the dark, empty space that echoes with the sound of his footsteps. We follow him into the office, through it, up the stairs, and into his apartment.

Once the door shuts behind us, Eddy stands in front of us, arms folded across his chest. "Who's Tara," he demands. "What's this help you need, and where's Francis?"

"Long story," I say.

There's a faint flicker in Eddy's eyes—amusement? "When Francis is involved, it usually is." He gestures at the couch I used as a bed the last time I was here. "Have a seat." He takes a chair across from us. "So," he says to me, leaning forward, his elbows on his knees, "the long story."

"Well," I say. "Remember when Francis and I showed up?"

He nods. I tell him briefly about life with crazy Gran before I met Francis. I give him a quick rundown about running away and learning how to live on the street, and then about meeting

Francis, about traveling around with him—just the bare bones. Only once does Eddy interrupt, when I relate the story Francis told me about running away to join the circus.

"He told you that?"

"That's what he said."

"Hm," is all he says.

I continue, explaining how Francis taught me the game, listing all the places I can remember us visiting. "Then we ended up at your place," I say. "After that, Francis decided to head east."

I tell him about the last day, about Francis wanting me to lift more than one item at a time, which I'd never done before—how it felt off-balance, out of whack. I describe the end: the angry vendor, the panic that froze me, the man grabbing my wrist tightly and not letting go. How I looked up and saw Francis standing and watching—the flash of hope: Francis could save me if he wanted to. How he turned his back, walked away, left me high and dry, then Tara/Deryn materializing beside me.

After I finish, Eddy is quiet for a while. Then he says, "It's not entirely true."

"What?"

"What he told you, how we met. For starters, we didn't meet at the Ex. And he didn't run away."

"He didn't?"

"No." He shakes his head. "He was taken, although I don't know if you can be taken if no one's holding on to you."

"What do you mean?"

"Well, from what he told us, his dad was out of the picture," Eddy says. "And his mother was a real piece of work. When she was sober, which wasn't often, she hit him because he reminded her of his old man. When she was drunk, she hit him because he wasn't his old man—he wasn't old enough to get out there and earn her some real money. 'What use are you?' she'd say to him."

"How do you know this?"

"I was with the circus," he says, as if this should be self-evident. "A tumbler. My mother and father, their parents, they were circus people all the way back.

"We were at this tiny place, Palookaville—I can't remember the name—in Iowa, I think, or Illinois, one of those 'I' states. It was a big deal when the circus pulled in to those places. They didn't have much going on besides drinking beer and playing chicken in cars on the back roads late at night.

"We were in that town two, three nights, and this kid is always showing up after the show, coming out of the shadows when we're getting packed up. I get talking to him—he's about my age. He's not so interested in the midway and the rides, there's some other draw for him. It turns out he's really interested in the elephants, so I take him over to Lucky, who's short a helper because, well, you know—he got that part right. The elephants seem to like the kid. He's cool around them, calm. He's not going to put them on edge. So, we talk about it and tell him, given what he's told us about the situation at home, he can come with us when we leave town if he wants to. When we pack up and leave, he comes too. So, he didn't so much run away as we took him in. If we hadn't offered, I don't know, he might still be there in Palookaville."

"His mom didn't call the cops, or go looking for him?"

"Who knows if she even noticed? I mean, yeah, eventually, but when? When the booze wore off? No, no one came looking for him. Or maybe it was like your gran—maybe his mother didn't want to deal with the cops." Eddy shrugs.

"Anyway, he fit in with us. We became his family. We travelled together for—" Eddy looks up at the ceiling "—six, seven years? And then he had that accident, and after, I don't know. I've heard the general outline of the story but never the particulars. Me, well, you can only work as a tumbler for so long. It wears the body out. I blew out a knee, ripped a tendon in my left leg, tore a rotator cuff. So, there I was, late twenties, ready for the scrap heap." He chuckles humourlessly.

He could have stuck with the circus, Eddy says, worked behind the scenes, done odd jobs, worked as a roustabout, maybe even moved into the business side of the operation. "Turns out I have a knack for it." Instead, he says, he'd met someone. On a layover in Toronto once. A friend of a friend. "Ran an antiques store. A *real* antiques store."

They started talking. The friend's friend—Iain—showed Eddy around auction houses, estate sales. Eddy found it absorbing—objects he'd never seen or conceived of before, he says, bone china, crystal, silver. Eddy's own family had never owned those kinds of things. "As you know, when you're moving around all the time you learn to carry only the essentials, you make do with what you have." Then he found himself in Iain's place, and it was stuffed to the rafters with things he'd never imagined existed. "Sterling silver toothpick holders—who needs a sterling silver toothpick holder?"

They hit it off. "He was a wonderful guy." Eddy smiles, remembering. "Smart, funny. Once he trusted you, he was really generous." That was the beginning. After a while Eddy started working in the store, learning the ropes. "And that," he says, "is how I ended up here."

"So, when did Francis—?" I ask. "When did you guys meet up again?"

Eddy looks at me, then his gaze slides away. After a minute he says, "By the time he showed up again I'd been working with Iain for a couple of years. I was a quick study. I guess all the time in the circus had taught me to think on my feet, plus, as I said, I seem to have a knack for business. I picked up a lot from Iain, from people he dealt with, collectors he knew, the people who hang around the antique world who are fanatic about specific objects or eras.

"Iain got sick." He gets quiet. I figure he's finished talking, but then he continues, "really sick. Associates disappeared, people who we thought were our friends evaporated." The equity in the store was all Iain had; he needed to access it to stay afloat, Eddy says. "We talked about liquidating the inventory, but it was going to be painful, we'd have to take a loss on most of it because we needed the cash fast. Iain couldn't work—could barely get out of bed most days." They were struggling.

"And then one day Francis walks into the store. 'Eddy!' he says, 'Boy-o, are you a sight for sore eyes!'" I can hear Francis's voice, upbeat, cheerful.

"He stopped and looked around. He says, 'I heard you were in the antiques business. Didn't believe it.' Then he grinned like the cat that ate the cream. 'Decided I had to see for myself—and here you are!' He swung his arms wide, taking in the whole store."

They talked about the circus, the old days. Francis gave Eddy a quick run-down of his life, told him about his adventures in the game, showed him pictures of the family, asked Eddy how business was.

"I told him things were fine, we were doing great, sales were strong. But he didn't buy it," Eddy says. "He gives me this look and says, 'I got eyes in my head, Eddy. I can see things aren't great. There's dust everywhere. You haven't moved much inventory in a long time. Why are you lying to me? I thought we were friends.'

"Maybe I was tired," Eddy says. Or maybe it was the bad news they'd had about Iain's diagnosis that morning—whatever the reason, it all spilled out. He told Francis the store was on its last legs. He told Francis about Iain, how it wasn't only the store that was on the line. Eddy was going to lose his partner too.

"He listened real closely," Eddy says. "You know the way he can sometimes lock onto something and give it his full attention. There was no kidding around, no jokes. Then he said, 'I'm sorry to hear that, Ed.' And pats me on the shoulder. I figured that'd be the end of it. He'd shake my hand, walk out the door the way so many people had, and it'd be the last I'd see of him."

Instead, he said, "'Excuse me,'" Eddy tells us. "'Going to poke around in here for a minute or two. Just ignore me.'" And he wandered off into the store. Eddy was going to go with him, show him around, pull out some of the best items, but the phone rang and Eddy was distracted for a while. He could hear thumps and bumps, a chest being opened, chairs being shifted around, drawers being opened and shut, a heavy object being dragged across the floor.

Eddy finished the call, and Francis reappeared. "'I might be able to help,' he says, 'No promises, mind you, but I may know some interested parties. I'll make a couple of calls, see if I can stir up some interest. That okay with you?' I said sure, any help gladly accepted. Then he was gone."

He came back a few days later with money. "Cash on the barrel," Eddy says. "Good money, too." With Francis's help, Eddy moved most of the rest of his inventory. "Not all of it, but close. I will always be indebted to him for that."

He's quiet for a while, thoughtful. When he starts talking again the words are measured. "Francis was there at the end, on the day of Iain's funeral, standing beside me. And then he drove me back to his place—the place where Francis was staying temporarily while he was in town—he said, 'You don't want to be going back to your apartment right now, Ed. All those memories. Let's get you a new place.' And he did that, too. When I tried to thank him, he wouldn't listen. 'I was stuck once and you helped me out,' he said. 'This is what friends do.'"

Eddy took the money remaining from the sale of the inventory—Iain had left it all to him—and looked around. "I realized running a store was hugely expensive. Why did I need a storefront when I could just as easily work out of where I lived, provided where I lived had the storage I needed? The store wasn't important; my contacts were what mattered." By then he wasn't selling to the public, anyway, he was mostly selling to other dealers and to collectors. When the warehouse came available, he thought about the situation and decided to move into transshipping.

"Transshipping?" I say.

Eddy glances at Deryn, then looks straight at me. "I help people *place* items," he says in a slow, deliberate way. "And I help other people find those items."

"'Place?'"

"Like what you and Francis brought me."

"Oh," I say as his meaning registers, that what Francis called *the provenance* of some of our inventory might be murky—that's what Eddy deals in.

"I didn't need to be out scouring the markets," he continues, "the markets could come to me, and Francis was one of the first to pay a call. He stands in the loading area and says, 'Nice place you have here, Ed. Real nice. I hope it works out for you.' He came back a few times afterwards with items to sell me. A lot of it was barely worth my time, but once in a while he showed up with quality pieces. He'd come and go, show up without warning, never hung around long. I never knew when he'd appear, and when he did, I never knew how long he'd stay. There was a period when I didn't see him for a couple of years, and then he showed up with you."

"Have you seen him since then?" I ask.

He shakes his head. "Nope."

"Do you have his phone number?"

"I do. But the last time I called, he didn't pick up. I left a voicemail, but he hasn't been in touch."

"Do you know anyone who might know where he is?" Deryn asks.

"Why?" Eddy asks. He looks at her almost challengingly.

Deryn looks at me.

I haven't told Deryn what I'm really after. I'm not going to tell Eddy, either. I'll tell him what I told her, a story to pull on the heartstrings, as Francis might say.

"I want to ask him why he dumped me," say, putting feeling into the words the way I saw Francis do when he was working a toff. "I thought we were friends, partners, and then he sets me up and walks away, leaving me to take the fall. If it weren't for her—" I look at Deryn "—someone might have called the cops. I might have ended up in big trouble."

He leans back, thinks about this. Then he says, "Maybe. I'd have to make some enquiries." He turns to Deryn. "What about you?" he asks. He sounds suspicious.

"What about me what?" she replies.

"What's your involvement?"

"She got me out of there after Francis ditched me," I tell him.

"I'm a friend of Frankie's," Deryn says, meeting his gaze steadily. "Like you."

Eddy's expression is hard to decipher. "Okay," he says, after a moment. "Give me your number," he tells me.

"It'll have to be hers," I say. "I don't have a phone."

Deryn gives him her number.

"Right," he says, "I'll ask around, see what I can find out. For old time's sake."

"Thanks, Eddy."

"Sure thing," he says gruffly.

14.

DERYN AND I HAVE TO figure out our next step. "Can't just wait around on his call," she says. We're sitting in the car, up the street from Eddy's.

Then she says, "I know somebody who might be able to help." She pulls out her phone, scrolls through it, and calls someone.

"Norm," she says. "Deryn. Hi. Yeah. Not bad—you?" She listens, nodding, then says, "Norm, I have a small favour to request. . ."

She asks Norm, who must deal with cars and with drivers' licenses, to see if he can find any information on a Francis Person. "Yeah, I know," she says with a low laugh. "Probably not his real name. What's the likelihood, eh? Okay, anything you can find would be a big help. Yup. Thanks, Norm." She hangs up. "Good. Maybe he can turn something up. Worth a shot." Then she turns and looks at me. "Now what?"

I stare back at her. I have no idea. I'm only along for the ride until we find Francis.

"Yeah," she says, taking in my expression. "I know. Why am I asking you?" She drums her fingers on the steering wheel. After maybe a minute she says, "I think our best bet is to find a place to land and sort through what we know."

She turns the key in the ignition and pulls onto the road.

We end up at a family-run motel, scruffy on the outside, but once we're inside the room is clean, and, as Deryn says, "The price is right." She sits on one of the twin beds and opens her laptop. "Here's what we know," she says, and starts making a list.

The call comes later, after we get back from picking up tacos for dinner. She's at work on her laptop and I'm scribbling in a notebook when the phone rings. On our drive back to the motel, Deryn suggested I write about my time with Francis. "Not for anyone else to read necessarily," she said, "just to help you understand."

At first, I resisted, coming up with reasons not to, then it started to make sense to me. I asked if I could have a notebook and a pen. She bought them for me at a corner store that sold phone cards and candies I didn't recognize from other countries—somewhere Asian, I think—and I started jotting down my recollections when we got back to the motel.

Deryn answers the phone and listens for a couple of seconds, says, "Sure," then passes it to me. "Eddy."

When I answer, he asks, "How you doing?"

"Okay," I say.

"I have a number for you." He rattles it off and I write it down in my notebook. "Tell her I sent you. She's expecting your call."

After we say goodbye, I give Deryn the phone number. "Who's it for?"

"He didn't say. He just said 'she.'"

"Toronto area code. What do you want to do?"

A moment's pause. "Call her. See her."

She shrugs. "Go ahead." I dial. A woman answers. Her voice is low, even. "You're the one looking for Francis?" she asks.

"Yes."

She gives me an address. I jot it down and pass it to Deryn. She says, "Tell her we could be there any time tomorrow. It'll take us about an hour, depending on traffic. Ask her how ten works for her."

"The door will be open," the woman says.

Next morning, we leave at around nine. The address the woman gave me turns out to be on a street of storefronts where Korean convenience stores, with stands of vegetables outside, sit beside fabric stores and second-hand clothing stores, mixed with butchers, nail salons, and old hardware stores. The signs here are in different languages, and I hear a mix of languages in the snippets of conversation going on when I climb out of the car.

I look around. It's a busy part of town, the sidewalks crowded with people, folks going into stores, sitting in cafes. I could probably take off if I wanted to, and I'm not convinced Deryn would care. I mean, she can go see this woman on her own, get the information. But it does feel like with her help I'm getting closer to Francis, and my knapsack and the photograph. I decide I'll stick with her a little longer, see what happens.

There's a door beside a fortune-telling store's front entrance. When I pull on the handle, the door is open, like the woman said it would be. Inside, there's a stairway, and at the top of the stairs there's another door, also open. I knock anyway, to announce our arrival. "Come in," calls the flat voice from the telephone yesterday.

I walk through the doorway into a bright room, full of light streaming through uncurtained windows.

There's not much furniture: a couch, a pair of matching armchairs, a small, round table in chipped, dark wood—but it's all clean and orderly. The couch and chairs are covered in bone-coloured fabric almost the same tone as the light-coloured walls. Bright woven throws hang over the arms of the couch, and there are a couple of colourful embroidered pillows, too. At the far end of the room, books of all shapes and sizes crowd shelves. Across the room, a person sits at a desk, their back to me.

While I scan the place, the person at the desk keeps writing. After a while she turns around and examines me and Deryn, who's standing behind me. The time she takes looking us over gives me a chance to observe her.

It's hard to tell how old she is. She could be twenty-five, she could be in her late thirties. She has a long, unlined face, and clear, alert eyes that give the impression she doesn't miss much. There's a seriousness to her, a heavy presence. Her dark hair is cut short. She wears jeans, a pale grey t-shirt, and over it, an embroidered shirt bleached and softened with age. Something about her—her reserve, her expression—seems like the echo of someone I've met before, but I can't place her. Someone remembered. Someone from my previous life?

Our eyes meet. For some reason—maybe the suggestion of humour in her eyes—I smile at her automatically. Her gaze glides over to Deryn, who's moved forward to stand beside me.

She examines Deryn for a while, then looks back at me. "You must be Frankie," she says, in her curiously uninflected voice.

My eyes meet hers. "Yes."

"But that's not your real name, is it?"

I glance sideways. Deryn's watching me, waiting for the answer. I look back to the woman at the desk.

For a beat, I hesitate. Is there any point in denying it? "No," I say.

"Okay," she says, as if she's satisfied, as if I—Frankie-who-is-not-Frankie—have passed some sort of test.

"Come in," she stands up, indicating the two armchairs. She sits down in the centre of the couch, I sit in an armchair on one side, and Deryn sits in the other one.

"So, Francis," she says simply.

"Yes."

"Why?"

I give her a short version. She draws her long legs up so she's sitting cross legged, her hands folded in her lap. When I've finished talking, she keeps sitting there for a while, scrutinizing me. Then she turns to Deryn. I get the impression she feels Deryn's presence is an intrusion. "And you?"

"Me what?" asks Deryn.

"What do you want from Francis?"

"Nothing. I'm here to help Frankie find him."

"That's kind of you." Her tone is ambiguous.

"I guess I've had a similar experience," Deryn says. "I understand why she'd want to talk to him, figure out what went on."

The woman stares, then shifts her attention back to me.

"How old are you?" she asks. "Sixteen?"

"Fifteen," I tell her.

"Ah," she says, lifting her chin a bit. She looks at me for a moment, weighing something, it seems. She takes a deep breath.

15.

MY NAME IS PASCALE, SHE BEGINS, speaking slowly, carefully.

When she says this, a faint recollection stirs, but as she keeps talking in her low, quiet voice, I have to lean in to hear her, and I forget the tickle of memory.

She says she was older than me when she met Francis, eighteen. It had begun two years before, when she left home at sixteen. Her parents had split up a couple of years earlier, and she was living with her mother. When a new boyfriend walked into her mother's life, it became crowded and uncomfortable at home. Pascale was seeing someone, Leo. Her stepfather hated Leo, and made her life really uncomfortable, so when Leo suggested she move in with him, she did. Her mother protested, but not too much, and her stepfather shut her mother down, "She's a grown-up," he said. "Let her figure it out." She felt cut off from her mother, she says, the person who had been the one constant in her life. I know that feeling.

Leo was a musician. What this meant, she tells us, was he slept all day and hung out in bars at night. He made his money dealing on the side.

When they were first together, he was thoughtful, romantic. He'd bring her flowers, write songs for her. It's an old story, but she hadn't heard it, or if she had, she didn't think it applied to her. After they moved in together, he started changing. Not immediately and not totally—there was still enough sweetness to keep her coming back, and after the first time he hit her, he apologized, but over time he hit her more and more often, and harder.

She thought about leaving, but everything she owned was in their apartment—her life was there—she wouldn't have enough money to replace her things if she just up and left—and where was she going to go? She couldn't go back to her mother's—her stepfather had made that clear.

Listening to her, I remember what it was like at Gran's as she grew more and more extreme—quoting scripture all the time, pulling the curtains on the windows because she was sure we were being watched—how I stayed because I didn't know what else to do, where else I could go. Every other option available to me would blow up my life, Gran's life. And yet, the longer it went on, the more it felt like I was falling further and further into a dark hole.

Pascale was working at a club, and Leo started demanding she give him all her tips. You don't make much in those jobs, she says, not even minimum, so the tips were what she lived on, what they lived on. One day she pushed back, and it was the first time she ended up in hospital.

She told the hospital staff she'd fallen off her bike, that was the reason for the cracked rib and the bruise on her face. When she left the hospital, she was not going to go back to him. She called a friend, who let her crash at their place.

Leo tracked her down and showed up there. He said, "I was drunk baby, I didn't mean it. It wasn't me; it was the booze. It'll never happen again." He kept promising over and over it would never happen again, crying. She believed him. She thought it was only one bad night. If she could simply do the right things and not upset him, everything would all be all right.

But a couple of months later it wasn't. He accused her of seeing someone else—a guy at work. "How could I?" she asked, when he knew where she was every minute of the day. She told him she wasn't seeing anyone. This only made him angrier. "Are you calling me a liar?" He threw her against the fridge. Hands, fists—he came at her so hard she had bruises all over her arms the next day from trying to keep him off. She snuck out of the apartment while he was sleeping it off with only the clothes on her back.

She wasn't going back to her friend's place—that would put her friend in danger. She asked around at work. A friend of one of the bartenders was looking for a roommate. She let Pascale move in.

But Leo showed up at the club a week later and acted out a scene from the old playbook, "I love you. Please come back." Except she wasn't having any of it. He goes apeshit, starts pushing her around, and when the bartender gets between them, Leo starts whaling on him, too. The place was trashed, the cops were called, and she was out of a job.

There was a regular at the club the night she was fired, Callum, a handsome guy, dark hair, blue, blue eyes. He was in his late twenties or early thirties, a moderately big spender, nothing dramatic, just steady. He was pleasant to the staff, knew all their names, made entertaining small talk, nothing too personal. He was a generous tipper.

A couple of days later the bartender called her, "Need a job?"

It turned out Callum was asking.

She figured she had nothing to lose by listening to what Callum had to say. If she didn't like what he was offering, she could say no and walk away.

She said sure and the bartender gave her his phone number.

She phoned Callum.

"Great to hear from you," he said, all friendly. He had a soft voice, easy on the ears. "Let's get together. I have an opportunity that might interest you."

She was skeptical, but she figured it couldn't hurt to hear him out. She didn't have to commit to anything. He named a bar in Yorkville, old, dingy, but familiar. Callum suggested they meet there the next night.

They sat in a booth. "My treat," he said. "What'll you have?" She was broke, so against her better judgment she let him buy her a ginger ale and a burger.

"This opportunity," he said once the food and drinks had arrived, "I know some men who work pretty high-pressure jobs—lawyers, CEOs, businessmen—influential people. Sometimes they're in town for a night, and all they want to do is kick back and relax, spend time talking to a smart, attractive young lady like yourself," he told her. "Now I admit—" he spread his hands wide, grinned "—mostly they want to do the talking, and they want you to do the listening, but they're prepared to pay for your time." He named an amount that surprised her.

"Just to talk?" It sounded too good to be true.

He nodded. "Just to talk."

She paused. "I have to think about it."

"Sure." Callum said. "You think about it. You have my number." He stood up and dropped a bunch of twenties on the table without seeming to count them. "I'll let you get on thinking about it. No pressure. Give me a call, let me know." He flashed her a smile and then he left.

She had an impulse to reach out, grab the twenties, count out enough to cover the bill, and pocket the rest, but that felt like it would be stealing, so she finished eating and left.

On the walk home, she thought how carelessly and casually he'd dropped the cash, and how great it would be to have so much money you could be that off-hand with it. She was always worrying about money. Her first thought in the morning was, how much money do I have? How much do I need to get through the day? How can I get more? These questions cycled through her mind all day, every day.

She thought about listening to men talk. She'd listened to Leo, and all she'd ended up with was bruises. Then she thought about doing it and making the amount of money Callum had mentioned, and she asked herself, how hard could it really be? She figured she could do it for a while and be looking for a job on the side, and once she found a job, she could walk away from the men and Callum, and it all seemed to make sense.

So, she called Callum and left a message, "Okay."

He phoned her back almost immediately. "Great," he said. "Now we have to dress you up. These guys like upscale places. They want to take you out, treat you right. You can't go to these places in jeans and a t-shirt. I have some friends. . ."

"I can't afford expensive clothes."

"I'll front you the money," he said. "Think of it as me betting on a sure thing. I have confidence in you. You can pay me back later when you're flush. You'll have fun."

She wasn't sure about all this.

"I understand," Callum said. "We'll take it slow. Try it once and see how you feel about it. If you don't like it, we'll call it quits."

The first time wasn't bad. Callum gave her an outfit to wear—dark slacks and matching jacket, pretty boring. The guy she met was an older man, about her stepfather's age. A banker in town for a conference, he said, and it was true, all he really wanted was someone to talk to. She met him at the Royal York. Callum had described him to her. She saw him sitting in the lobby and went up and introduced herself to him. They had cocktails at a nearby bar, and then he took her to a high-end steak house—"I'm an old-fashioned guy," he said, "I like it simple, meat and potatoes." He told her about his work, his family. He said he had a daughter about her age going into pre-med. He asked what she wanted to do when she was older. She said she really didn't know. He patted her hand and said, "You're a smart young lady. I'm sure you'll figure it out." After dinner he asked where he could drop her off. And that was it.

That wasn't hard, she thought. This is going to be easier than she'd figured.

The second time. . .the second time it was a young guy. He said he was V.P. of something-or-other with a multinational company she'd never heard of, head office in Hong Kong or Bangkok—she can't remember all he told her, everything coming out in a rush. Amped up on coke, speed, she couldn't tell what—his eyes bright and sharp, he was all over sharp: his hair was precisely styled, his suit was beautifully tailored, his shoes were buffed to a glittering shine.

When they met, he grabbed her elbow and took her in in a single up and down look, proprietary, predatory almost. Like he owned her, like she was another accessory to go with his shiny shoes, his Rolex watch, his French cuffs.

He guided her to the bar and ordered cocktails for them both. She said she'd rather have a ginger ale, but he smiled again—his eyes didn't smile—and he said, "Humour me," in a tone with no humour in it.

He was creeping her out. She excused herself to go to the washroom and phoned Callum from one of the stalls. She told him it wasn't going well, the guy was weird.

"Carlson?" he said. "He's just a hot-shot. I'll have a word with him, tell him to dial it back. Give me a moment, then go back. If he's still bothering you later, give me a call and I'll come pick you up."

She waited long enough for a call, then she went back

Carlson looked apologetic when she slid into her seat. "Sorry if I've been too intense," he said. He lifted his phone off the bar and gave it a shake to indicate he'd heard from Callum. "I have a lot on my plate at the moment, a big deal going through, although I'll admit, even at the best of times I'm sort of wired. So, let's relax and have a pleasant time," he said and pushed a drink towards her. "This'll take the edge off." He did seem more mellow. She took a sip of the cocktail, and then another.

When she woke up, someone was slapping her face. She tried to push them away, but she was groggy, coming out of what felt like a deep sleep, trying to make sense of what was going on, the world hazy except for the sharp stinging sensation where she'd been slapped.

As she surfaced, the fog lifted from her brain and the room around her came into focus, someone slapped her again. She tried to say no, but her tongue was thick and her mouth was stupid. And when she finally figured out what was happening, she saw it was Carlson hitting her, and all the time he was growling, "Wake up. Wake up."

"I'm awake," was all she could get out. Her mouth was dry.

"About time," he said.

She started to cry. "Shut up," he said, and drew his hand back to hit her again, but someone reached out, grabbed his wrist, and stopped him.

Then a voice she knew, soft, and soothing. "No bruises on the face or arms. Stick to the body." Callum stepped forward from where he'd been standing, out of sight. "We don't want to damage the goods." He leaned in close, his face right beside hers, his breath hot on her cheek. "Do we, Pascale?" he asked, dropping his voice to almost a whisper.

She's not sure how long Callum kept her in the room—long enough for her to memorize the greasy purple wallpaper, the ratty lamp they left on all the time, which only lit a tiny corner of the room, the wobbly bedside table, the smell of the place: sweat, cigarette smoke (Carlson smoked constantly), and another moldy, mildewy smell, the crummy, slippery synthetic dark green bedspread someone sometimes tossed over her but mostly didn't. She listened hard for a sound that would help her figure out where she was, but all she could hear was the low hum of air conditioning and, once a day, the loud jangle of a heavy vehicle—a streetcar?—slamming into something in the road. Whenever Callum went out, Carlson was there. Whenever Carlson went out, Callum was there. She was never alone.

She fell asleep, she doesn't know for how long. They had the curtains pulled so she never knew if it was day or night. When she woke up, she was hungry.

Callum went away and came back with food. Hamburgers, fries, a coffee. Even now the smell of hamburger makes her retch, she says.

The room had a table with a TV on it. Callum put the food on the table beside the TV, he sat on the end of the bed and Carlson leaned against the wall and they ate the food and smirked at her. She was so hungry she would have eaten the ketchup in the little bags, but they didn't give her anything.

When he was done eating, Callum stood up and came over to where she was, and he sat on the bed. There was one bag of food left, giving off the oily smell of hamburger and deep-fried French fries. Callum dangled the bag above her and said, "You belong to me." He bent over and pushed his face so close to hers she could see the beginnings of dark stubble on his jaw. "And not in some cutesy pop song way. I *own* you—got it?"

When she didn't answer, he glanced over his shoulder. On that signal, Carlson straightened up and came over and stood behind him.

"Say it," Callum told her. "Say, 'You own me.'"

"You own me," she said flatly.

He shook his head. "Like you mean it," Callum said. "Say it, 'You own me.'"

"You own me," she said with as much feeling as she could manage. Her eyes stung with tears.

He flicked his hand at Carlson, and she heard him move away. Callum gave her the bag of food. It was gross, and the best meal she'd ever eaten, both at the same time.

Other times Callum was gentle—washing her face, brushing her hair. He'd get up close when he did this. Sometimes he'd stroke her cheek. "Poor Pascale," he'd say. "Poor, poor Pascale."

She never knew which Callum it was going to be, kind Callum or cruel Callum.

She doesn't know how long it went on that way, but one day Callum went out. Maybe an hour later he came back, and he was carrying a plastic bag, a big plastic bag, not food this time. He pulled out a dress, skimpy, made of some synthetic material, it had a colourful flower pattern in bright tones. He handed it to her. "Put it on," he said.

She pulled it on over her head. It wasn't a dress she would ever buy; the neckline plummeted, the design of the bodice pushed her breasts up. The hem skimmed the top of her thighs. She stood in front of them feeling exposed, uncovered.

"Stand up straight," Callum said.

She took a breath and stood taller.

"Come on, come on," he barked irritably. "Shoulders back, chest out."

She did her best.

He walked over and circled her, his face close to hers. "The first thing you need to know is, no one's looking for you. No one. No posters, no news reports, nothing." He stopped in front of her and made a sad face, held it for a second. Then his usual bored expression returned. "The second thing is, you're going to work for me. You do a good job," he said, "I'll take good care of you." He smiled, reached up, and stroked her cheek. She flinched away. "You don't—" he continued in his lazy, silky voice "—I'll get rid of you." He hit her hard. Her head jerked sideways and the side of her face burned. He turned and walked away. "And no one'll be looking for you then, either."

~

She's not sure how long she worked for Callum. She's tried to figure it out—maybe a year, maybe a couple of months more, parts of it are indistinct.

First, in the house. It turned out they were holding her in a sprawling, old Victorian place that had been turned into a rooming house at some point. There were a dozen girls in there. On the ground floor at the back was a kitchen, separate from the girls' rooms. The clients never went there. Callum kept the place stocked. That's where they ate.

It's where she got to know some of the other girls in passing. Some were younger than her, runaways Callum had picked up on the street. Some were foreign; it was hard to understand the foreign ones; she figures they came from Russia or Eastern Europe. A lot of the time they seemed stoned, doped up. Sometimes she felt stoned. She assumes Callum kept them stoned. She doesn't know how he did it, maybe in the food. It was better for him that way, easier to keep them in line, and better for them, too, in a way. Being stoned was similar to being asleep and dreaming—a bad dream, admittedly, but maybe you'd wake up one day, out of the dream, into something else, maybe something better.

There was a lot of turnover among the girls. Callum had other places, always in rough parts of town so no one paid much attention to all the coming and going. He'd move the girls around, so they were never in the same place long and they never got to know each other well. Callum and Carlson were the only people they saw regularly; there were other men—always men—to keep them in line if Callum or Carlson weren't around. The clients came to the house. They paid Callum. He pocketed the money. He told the girls not to try anything stupid—there were cameras everywhere.

After a while, he moved her onto the street, onto the track. She doesn't know why. Maybe because she was talking with the other girls too much.

There were good things about being on the track and bad things. She liked the fact she was outside—she didn't feel as much of a prisoner. After being stuck inside for months, she liked to be out in real light, knowing what time of day (usually night) it was. She liked the weather, how one day it was overcast and misty, and the next day it could be crystal clear. She loved looking at the sky, how it was always different. She even liked the rain, because inside it couldn't rain.

But the men were scarier. She hated getting in cars. At the house, someone was always there; if a client was too rough, Carlson or one of the other guys Callum had on staff would show up and escort him away. On the track, Callum had guys keeping an eye on them and collecting the money, but what could those guys do when she climbed in a car? On the street no one had their backs.

That's where Francis saw her—on the street.

It was late October—she knew this because there were Hallowe'en decorations everywhere—cold and wet. Callum dropped her off. There'd been an incident or exchange between them (she couldn't remember precisely what it had been about) and he was pissed off at her. It was miserable out, late afternoon, and she was tired. He climbed out of the car, came around to the passenger side and grabbed her arm and dragged her out of the car. Maybe he felt he could do that then because there wasn't anyone around. Who'd be out on a night like that except johns? He was holding her wrist really tight, and she was trying to pull away from him. He gave her a quick slap—one, two—and snarled, "Quit it. Get out there—" He jerked his chin toward the street and shoved her in that direction. "No funny business," he said, and climbed back in the car and shut the door.

A couple of minutes later Francis pulled up in his truck, leaned over, and rolled down the passenger-side window. He tipped his head sideways to make eye contact.

She went and leaned on the window. "What are you interested in?" she asked.

"Just talk."

She laughed. As if. "Oh, yeah?"

He pulled out a fifty-dollar bill and set it on the passenger seat.

"Let's see how much conversation this covers," he said.

"'Conversation.'" She figured he was kidding, but she opened the door, grabbed the fifty, and climbed in. He drove to a 24-hour donut shop a couple of kilometers away and parked. Then, before he got out, he turned to her and said, "I'm serious. I only want to talk. I'll buy you a coffee—" he tilted his head in the direction of the donut shop, its windows bright in the dark and drizzle "—if you're not comfortable, we'll call it quits. I'll drive you back or put you in a cab and send you back—whatever you like."

It wasn't the normal transaction, but she had the fifty bucks, so what did she have to lose?

They went in. He bought her coffee and a sandwich—"You're looking kind of peaky." Which was what her mother used to say to her when she was a kid and not feeling well, and then her mom would let her stay home from school and watch TV all day and drink ginger ale. She felt a catch in her throat when he said this. He sat down across from her.

"My name's Francis," he said. "How did a young woman like you get into this line of work?"

She thought, *are you kidding me?* But she didn't say that, didn't say much, told him she'd hit a rough patch a while back, but things were looking up recently, things were fine. He seemed disappointed; he shook his head. "I saw him hit you." His voice was low. "I have a daughter. I wouldn't want her to be treated that way."

The way he said it—softly and gently—and the way he looked at her, she broke down and started crying. She was so tired and so sad. And he sat there and passed her napkins to wipe her eyes and blow her nose, and looked around at the people who were watching, and he stared them down, calmly, until they looked away.

When her crying slowed down, he said, "Tell me about it," in a low voice.

She looked him over for a moment. Did he really have a daughter? Was he actually asking? Or was this another version of Callum's tricks, another man trying to trap her?

He spread his hands wide and leaned back. "That's okay," he said. "Not if you don't want to. I could see how it would be hard."

She told him everything—about Leo, about couch-surfing, about meeting Callum. She told him about Carlson, and waking up groggy in the room. She told him about the beatings. And how Callum could switch from kind to cruel in a blink. About the houses, the clients, and then Callum putting her on the street. And Francis just listened.

When she finished, they sat there, facing each other across the table. Then he said—really quietly—"I have a suggestion." It sounded more like a question than a statement. "You could stay with my wife and my daughter and me. I could take you there now. Wait—"

He stood up, cocked a finger, beckoned. She followed him to a payphone at the back of the place, he dropped some coins in, dialed a number.

Someone answered and he said, "Tam, I met someone who needs a place to stay, maybe for a while." Then he listened and after a while he said, "That's great. Could you tell her?"

He passed her the receiver and this woman says, "Hi, hello." She had a lovely voice, warm and friendly, with a hint of a drawl.

"Hi."

"Hi. I'm Tamsin, Francis's wife."

"I'm Pascale."

"He says you need a place to stay."

"Yeah."

"You're welcome to stay with us," she said. "It's not a big place, and there's four of us already. We don't live high on the hog, but if you need a place to bunk down, feel free."

She thought she might start crying again. All she could say was, "Sure. Thanks."

"Can you pass me back to my husband, please?"

She gave Francis the phone and he talked to Tamsin for a minute in a low murmur. After he hung up, he said, "So what do you think?"

"Can you give me a moment?"

He shrugged. "Sure. Take your time."

They walked back to the table where they'd been sitting. She tried to figure out what her choices were. If she said no and he took her back to where he'd picked her up, Callum might drop her somewhere else later that night, or the next night, and she'd never see Francis again. Then she thought, leaving with Francis was the first step in escaping from Callum, so she said, "I'll go with you."

"Glad to hear it," he said. They finished their coffees and she followed him back to the truck. It was a long drive to his place, and it was dark when they arrived. He lived in a dingy house in a semi-rural area past the city limits, not suburban, but not really country. They went down a long driveway, and her first impression was that these people didn't have much money: the aluminum siding on the house was dented and chipped, there was a scrubby front yard, a kid's bike lying by the side of the gravel driveway.

They went through a side door, into the kitchen, and Tamsin was sitting at the kitchen table. She was beautiful—long, blonde hair, delicate features.

The kitchen was a small room, one lamp hanging over a square table that would barely accommodate three people. The cupboards looked handmade and were painted a tired grey-green colour. It was all really clean, but with the faded, bleached look places get when they've been scrubbed and scrubbed for years and the paint is wearing thin. Old, chipped linoleum tiles on the floor; in some places the wood subfloor showed through.

The table had two places set, and Pascale could smell food. Tamsin smiled when they walked in and stood up to hug Francis. "I saved you some supper."

"You are a pearl of great price," he said, putting his arms around her. Pascale didn't know what that meant, but it sounded affectionate.

Then he said, "Pascale, this is Tamsin. But I guess you figured that out. Tamsin, Pascale."

"Take a seat," she said, waving at the empty chairs, "and help yourself. I hope you like spaghetti." After they ate, Tamsin took her into the room next door, the living room. It had a tiny TV, a chair, and a matching couch made up into a bed. "You get the sofa for tonight. I'll sort out sleeping arrangements tomorrow.

We'll leave the light on in the bathroom for you." Tamsin patted her on the shoulder. "Try and sleep. We'll talk in the morning."

It turned out Francis knew someone who knew someone, a friend of a friend, on the police force. Francis had what he called an 'ambivalent' relationship with the police, "but it's always wise to have an ally in the enemy camp," he said. He passed along some of what she'd told him to his contact. She'd told Francis where the houses were, what Callum and Carlson looked like, how it all worked.

Carlson was picked up and charged. So were a few of the other guys. The girls—some of them were as young as twelve. A few of the older ones were charged when the vice cops picked them up; the younger ones went into the Youth Justice System. Callum managed to get away. Maybe someone tipped him off.

Francis and Tam took her in for a while. They helped her navigate social services, find a safe place to live, get a job. They convinced her to take correspondence courses to finish her high school. Later, Francis taught her about antiques, collectibles. Helped get her started in the business.

Morning has turned to afternoon while she's been telling her story, and suddenly realization clicks into place: "You're the lady," I blurt out. It's all come back to me in an instant. "In the store. In the town. We stopped there once. You sent him to the guy with the stall in the market. Ray something. Your hair's different."

Her hand moves to her hair, almost unconsciously, it seems. She rubs the back of her neck.

"Ray Cooper," she says. "Yes, that was me. When Eddy called, I remembered you from the time the two of you dropped in the store. Now you know how I know Francis, I think you can understand why I'm. . .what you might call selective about who I put in touch with him," she says.

I look at Deryn, then back at Pascale. "He took care of me, too," I tell her. "I thought we were a team. I held up my end of the deal. I did things for him I knew were wrong and risky, and he set me up, and he walked out on me. Why? I thought he was my friend. Why did he leave me? That's what I want to ask him."

She's thoughtful for a moment. "All right," she says. "I'll let him know you want to talk to him. Eddy gave me your number. I can't make any promises, but I'll pass the message along."

I look at Deryn. She lifts her shoulders, a small movement—nothing else to be done. I look back at Pascale. "Thanks."

She unfolds her legs, stands up. Time to leave.

On the drive back to the motel I stare out the window. A shiver goes through me. That could have been me, I think, that girl on the street. If Francis hadn't been keeping an eye on me and stepped in, maybe it's what Beer Guy had in mind.

And like Callum told Pascale, no one would have been looking for me. No one would have noticed if I had disappeared.

16.

LATER THAT AFTERNOON, AFTER WE'VE finished lunch, we're back at the motel. Deryn's on her laptop, and I'm writing in my notebook again—her phone rings. She looks up, over the top of her laptop screen, nods for me to answer it.

"Frankie!" I recognize him immediately, the bounce in his voice, the exuberance.

"Hi," I say, cautiously.

"I hear you're looking for me."

"Yeah."

"What for?"

"I want to talk."

"About what?"

"What you did. You dumped me," I answer. I can hear the accusation in my voice. "You took off and left me there to deal with the fallout all by myself."

"Whoa, whoa, whoa," he says. "Cool and calm here, Frankie, my girl. No need to get bent out of shape. You haven't thought this one through: Am I likely to want to get together with someone who's going to give me an earful?"

"I just want to know," I say in a low voice.

"I know you do," he says, shifting into a patient and understanding tone. "And since I feel I owe you an apology, sure, let's get together. I have some conditions, though."

He tells me his conditions. He's willing to meet, he tells me, and I say I know how to get to Eddy's. "Smart girl," he says. "Always knew you were a sharp one. Let's meet there."

But I have to come during the day, he says, and I have to come alone. "No hangers-on," he specifies. "No companions. I'll be watching. I'll see you half a mile away, and if anyone's with you, you won't find me there when you arrive. I'll be miles away. And I will never agree to meet you again. Door closed, story finished, all that. Understand?"

"I understand."

He tells me what time to be there the next day. "Eddy's at noon tomorrow, by myself, no hangers-on," I repeat back to him.

"You got it. See you then." And the line goes dead.

When I put the phone down, Deryn shuts her laptop. "What's up?"

"Francis," I tell her. "He says he'll meet me. Noon—tomorrow at Eddy's."

"I heard."

"Alone, he says. Or I'll never see him again."

17.

SO, LATE THE NEXT MORNING, on a brisk, sunny day, I'm walking along the road to Eddy's. Deryn dropped me off about half a mile away from Lougheed's Haulage. She parked on the side of the road. "I'll wait here 'til you get back," she said, reclining her seat like she was going to take a nap.

I feel a bit nervous, a little light-headed. Will Francis be there? He said he would be, but a lot of the time Francis says what he thinks the other person wants to hear.

It comes back to me, what Deryn said—how something breaking in your life doesn't have to break you, you can learn from it.

What can I learn from what's happened that can help me here? I took a risk—leaving Gran's—and it was tough, but I survived. Right now, I'm nervous, but I've been nervous before and I'm still here. Don't let nervousness push you around, don't make decisions based on it. Figure out what's important, what it is you really need at the end of it all.

For me, now, it's my mom's photo. That's what I'm after. If I hold onto that thought, I should be able to handle this.

Eddy's warehouse comes into sight. I walk through the gap in the chain link fence and cross the lot, knock on the door, then step back so Francis can see me from upstairs, the way he said to. My heart is beating fast, and my stomach is knotted.

The kitchen window stares back at me blankly. It looks like no one's home, but I stay where I am and wait, and in a couple of minutes the door in front of me swings open, and out steps Francis with a spring in his step, smiling, his eyes bright. "Frankie, Frankie, Frankie," he says. "You are a sight for sore eyes."

I stand there watching him, everything I've wanted to say to him, everything I've wanted to ask him jumbled up in my head, and I'm trying to figure out where to start when a sound on my left startles me, and I turn to see someone stepping around the corner of the building. It's Deryn. She has her eyes fixed on Francis, like a hawk with its eyes fixed on its prey. She says, "So are you, Dad. So are you."

191. Found

18.

DAD? FROZEN, I STARE AT DERYN, trying to process what she's just said. She stands a couple of meters away, her eyes on Francis, her expression unreadable.

I look over at Francis—he's not smiling any more. He's got his eyes fixed on Deryn, his face a blank mask, all his hail-fellow-well-met good cheer gone, the playfulness erased.

"Derrie," he says slowly, as if he's trying to figure out a riddle. "Where'd you come from?" His voice is soft, quiet. "I was watching. I didn't see you following her."

Deryn laughs lightly. "I guess I'm my father's daughter." And in that moment, the pieces fall into place: why she's been so willing to help me, the echo I right this second hear in the way she speaks sometimes that reminds me of Francis: *I recognize the juncture where you find yourself.* Subtly embellished, with a bit of a flourish, like him.

"Learned a few things from you, picked up a few tricks," she continues. "How to run a variation on the old bait and switch." She steps over and stands beside me.

Francis looks at me, then back at Deryn. "So, you've been on my tail all this time?" he asks.

She gives a tiny shrug. "At the beginning, I knew where you were. Pascale texted Mom after you two showed up, but then

Mom collapsed again and I had to rush her to hospital, and by the time she was discharged, you were long gone.

"When Mom was better, I tried to reach Pascale to ask her to put me in touch with you, but you spooked her, Dad, showing up without warning. She wasn't answering my texts, so I went to her store. She'd left. Her business partner didn't know where she'd gone—she told me Pascale had started having nightmares after your visit. I guess it brought back a lot of memories. Pascale told her partner she needed to take a break; she was going to go visit a friend."

Francis scans the area, then jerks his head towards the door to Eddy's. "Let's take this inside."

"Sure," says Deryn.

I follow Francis, Deryn follows me. Francis shuts the door behind us; we go through the office and up the stairs to Eddy's place. It's pretty much the same as the last time I was here: chairs, roomy couch, kitchen at the other end of the space. It's cooler in here than it was in the parking lot, quiet.

Eddy's sitting at the kitchen counter at the other end of the room. He looks up when we walk in. "Oh," he says, "guests."

"Hope you don't mind, Ed," says Francis.

"Nope," Eddy replies. "No problem. I can go in the other room if you want."

"Nah. Why don't you join us? Couple of people here you might remember."

"Really?" Eddy stands up and walks over.

"Ed, this is Derrie," Francis rests his hand on Deryn's shoulder. "You've met her before."

"Derrie?" Eddy blurts in a tone of disbelief. "Really? The last time I saw you, you were—" he holds his hand barely hip-high.

"About five." Deryn says, smiling.

"That long ago?" Eddy frowns, considers. "Yeah, I guess."

"And Frankie you know."

Eddy grins at me. "Sure do. You manage to keep him in line and out of trouble?" he teases me. Then, "Have a seat," he says, gesturing at the couch and chairs.

When we're all seated—Deryn beside me on the couch, Francis and Eddy in the chairs—Francis leans forward, plants his elbows on his knees, and says to Deryn, "So, you were on my tail."

"Right. I retraced the route from last time, hoping I'd find you. I caught up with you in Enterprise. Then I watched for a while. I was trying to figure out what was going on, how to handle it. If I just showed up, I thought you might bolt—which, in the end you did. Plus, you had her along—" she tilts her head toward me. "I wasn't sure what was going on. I didn't want to complicate the situation, I didn't want a scene, didn't want any drama. More to the point, I did not want the cops involved, or Children's Services. I simply wanted to talk to you. I was right on the point of it in Kingston when you took off—leaving her in a pretty crummy situation, I might add." She glances at me, then back at him.

"I had to deal with that. I didn't want to up and leave her all on her own—I needed to get her out of there. If the cops had picked her up and started asking questions, things might have gotten messy. By the time I put out that fire, you'd disappeared. I could have tried to rush back to the motel immediately after you walked off, but I don't think Frankie would have gotten in the car with me right then."

They all look at me. Deryn raises her eyebrows. I think back to that time, how frozen I felt when he disappeared, how angry I was with her at first. I shake my head.

"And if I'd forced the issue and she'd made a fuss, it would have drawn attention, someone might have called the cops. I had to keep things locked down.

"By the time we made it back to the motel, you were gone.

Lucky for me, Frankie'd been paying attention." She gives my shoulder a squeeze. "Frankie and I, we did a little research, did a little detective work. She led me to Eddy; Frankie talked to Eddy; Eddy was in touch with Pascale. Frankie and I went and saw Pascale. She hadn't seen me since I was a kid, she didn't recognize me. I figured if Pascale knew what Frankie had been through, even if Pascale was having a bad time, she might be willing to help. Turned out I was right." Then she fixes her gaze on Francis. "It's time to come home, Dad. Mom needs you."

He frowns.

"It was a stroke," Deryn continues. "Turns out she's been having small ones for a while. She's going to get better. Maybe not all the way better, but the doctors say she's on the mend. She needs you, Dad."

She turns to me. "Something like this happened before with him," she says. Her expression clouds over. It feels like she's withdrawn inside herself. She looks down at the coffee cup in her hands. "After my sister died."

"Your sister?" I repeat.

She nods. "Phoebe." Her voice is warm. "My sister."

Francis says, "She was a beautiful girl wasn't she, Derrie?" His voice cracks.

"She was, Dad."

"She was." It's the first time Eddy's spoken since he sat down with us. We all look at him.

"And it was my fault," says Francis.

'Not your fault," says Eddy.

"For sticking my nose in."

"Francis," Eddy leans forward. "You couldn't know. You did the right thing."

"Dad." Deryn turns to face her father, her voice is urgent, her gaze locked on his face. "The cops said it wasn't your fault."

Francis blinks. Our eyes meet, then he looks away. "You know all about Pascale, right, Frankie? And Callum?"

"She told us."

"I saw her," he continues, "Pascale, on the street—this would have been—" he shakes his head "—almost twenty years ago. She reminded me of Phoebe, too. I saw him hit her. I guess I could have gone to the cops, but I've always had a. . .complicated relationship with them, dating from my circus days. You know, we'd pull into town and after that, every little thing that went wrong was our fault. So, I did what I did."

He falls quiet. After a moment he takes a deep breath. When he starts talking again it seems labored, difficult, like he's pulling the words from deep inside himself, a part he usually keeps hidden.

"I had a client, Rafael—almost a friend, I'd say. He was an interior designer, and he also collected for himself. He was always on the look-out for quite specific items and he had me keeping an eye out for him, too. If I saw an article I thought he might be interested in, I'd give him a call. One day, about six months after I helped Pascale get off the streets, I found a bookcase at an estate sale. He'd been looking for one like it for a while. I phoned him, described it. He told me how high he was willing to go for it. I acquired it for about three-quarters of that.

"So, I'm delivering this. I go to his place regularly, maybe every three or four months. This time I took Pheebes with me. I loved having her along," he says, smiling. "She was a smart kid, curious. Picked up ideas, information really quickly—like you. I told her I'd pass the business along to her when I retired. She'd laugh at me when I said that—no way she was going to drive around buying and selling people's left-overs. 'Left-overs' was exactly what she said." He gives a low chuckle. "She wanted to be a vet, help animals, live on a farm.

"This time we go to Rafael's, drop off the bookcase. He pays me, I pocket a reasonable but not extortionate profit. We chat a few minutes. Then Pheebes and I are heading home.

"Rafael lives out in the country. I'm driving along a concession road, come to a stop sign, stop, drive forward."

He stops, takes a deep breath. "He came out of nowhere," he says. "T-boned the truck. She was in the passenger's seat. Never had a chance." He stops. "It would have been better if. . ." His voice trails off, fades away.

"Callum?" I ask, after he's been silent for a few seconds.

His head jerks sharply in my direction, as if he'd wandered away from us in his mind, and my question is pulling him back into the present, away from a memory.

"Callum." He stares straight at me, but it's more like he's gazing through me at someone else. "I still don't know how he found me. The cops said maybe someone saw me talking to Pascale, or maybe someone saw us together later. Anyway, he walked away from the accident. Not a scratch on him. I had some broken ribs, a concussion, but Pheebes. . ." He shakes his head briefly.

"There was a trial." A sharp bark of laughter, a bitter sound. "A travesty. Turned out it was a bad intersection. There's a sign there now, right before you get to it; they put it up after the accident, 'Beware, high collision intersection.' Callum testified I'd run the stop sign, said he couldn't stop in time. Claimed he had nightmares about the whole episode, couldn't sleep, had whiplash, the whole nine yards. He was very convincing. Got off scot-free. He killed my daughter and never served a day." His voice is low, level, matter-of-fact—a current of anger coursing beneath the words.

"I wanted to kill him. I would have taken great satisfaction in beating him to a bloody pulp, or buying a gun and hunting him down, but Tam wept and reasoned with me, talked me out of it. She said Phoebe's death was bad enough, more violence wouldn't bring her back, and if I attacked him, I'd go to jail and she would have lost both of us.

"I went slightly nuts after that, I'll admit. I lost track of. . . things. It went on for a while. I was crazy with anger. Anger's bad—it can take over your whole life, everywhere you look, all you can see is anger, it colours everything."

He stops, as if he's tired, subsides into silence.

Deryn says to me, "He disappeared after that. Had a breakdown of some sort. There's a name for it—a type of amnesia, the doctors told us. He was gone for about six months. Mom found him through some of his associates." She looks over at Eddy. Their eyes meet. "Eddy helped. She tracked him down, found him psychiatric help. It took a while, but he seemed to get better."

Francis says, "When the dust settled, Pascale took Tam's side. Tam didn't want her to, but—" He raises his hands in a gesture of helplessness. "Funny how that happens; these situations push people into camps, for and against. Anyway, Pascale and I didn't—we weren't as close as we'd been." The coolness I sensed when we walked into the store that time. "But I'd drop in on her every now and then, see how she was doing.

"Eventually Callum was picked up on some charges that did stick. Maybe he crossed the wrong person—someone with clout. That was good. It took time, but Tam and I, we came to an understanding, opened up the lines of communication, as it were." He glances at Deryn. "With Derrie's help. We got back together.

"Then Callum was released. I knew when it was going to happen; one of the lawyers on the case who knew the whole story, he kept me in the loop—sub rosa, of course. I was there when they let Callum out. He didn't know. I followed him. Tam tried to talk me out of it, but I couldn't help myself.

"I had my eye on him; he had his eye on you," he says to me. "I saw you standing outside the Eaton Centre. It was freaking freezing. You looked—alone. You had your arms wrapped tight around you, like you were holding yourself together, barely. There was a quality about you that reminded me of Pheebes." He searches my face.

"Fierce," he says finally. "She had a fierceness about her." He takes a deep breath. "I saw Callum hanging around you. The guy outside the library, the guy in the alley."

"That was Callum?" I ask.

"That was Callum. And after what I'd seen with Pascale, I couldn't stand the thought of him getting his hands on you, you ending up working the street for him. But I wasn't going to take you home—not after what happened before. It felt too dangerous, like doing the same thing twice would be tempting fate. If I took you home and something happened—" He takes a deep breath, shakes his head. "Then Derrie calls me to say Tam had collapsed. That's when it all fell apart again, like after Pheebes. I came up with a solution. It was nuts, and I knew it was nuts, but I couldn't think straight—all I could think about was getting you away from him. And it worked, for a while, you know?"

He nods, to himself more than to me. I look at Deryn, Eddy, they're watching Francis.

"I kept you close as long as I could. But I knew it couldn't last. I could tell it was going to have to end eventually," he says. "I couldn't stand waiting for the end to come. It was always hanging over me. I was tired of expecting some official to turn up out of nowhere, knock on the motel room door, or sweep in without warning and pick us up at a market."

"Where's Callum now?" Deryn asks.

Francis's gaze moves to her, then to Eddy. A look passes between them. "Oh, Eddy and me, we sorted him." His mouth curves in a cold smile. "He won't be bothering anybody from now on."

"Dad?" Deryn says, alarmed.

"He's not dead," Eddy says to her. "We didn't kill him. Just, you know, helped him see the error of his ways. Made sure he couldn't pull the same garbage again."

Deryn looks at her father, frowning.

"Should have done it a long time ago, actually," Francis says thoughtfully. "Ah, well, better late than never, eh, Ed?"

"Long overdue," says Eddy.

"So, Eddy lied when he said he hadn't seen you since we dropped in?" I ask.

"I don't know about *lie*," Francis says.

"He lied," Deryn says to me.

"I lied," Eddy admits.

I turn to Eddy. "Why didn't you put us in touch with him?"

"Ah, well, the Edster." Francis jumps in. "He'll have his reasons. Probably didn't want to be responsible if it all went south, so he passed you on to Pascale. Let her be the gatekeeper. He prefers to keep out of sight, right?"

Eddy nods.

Francis is quiet for a while, then he starts talking again, this time in a conversational tone. "I know all about you, Frankie," he says. "I know your real name's Claire." I stare at him. "I asked around—some of the kids I saw leaving the places where you crashed. They started out all secretive, but you know me—I can usually finagle any information I'm after. They were broke, down on their luck; a hot coffee and a meal, strategically deployed, can get an incredible amount of information in those situations, as you know. I forget what lie I told them—long-lost uncle or some such. I knew where your grandmother lived."

"All along?"

"All along."

"That's kind of weird."

"Not really," he says. "I didn't want to scare you off by letting you know, but if something bad happened, if there was an accident, an emergency of some sort, I wanted the news to get back to your gran somehow. I told Pascale about her the time we dropped in, told her where your gran lived. I figured someone besides me should know."

"Why didn't Pascale tell me any of this, or Eddy?"

"Eddy didn't know the whole story. Some of it was Pascale's to tell, and I wasn't going to share it without her O.K. Pascale, she's protective of Tam, doesn't want her upset. Plus, after what she's been through, she doesn't like stirring things up, status quo is what she's driving for, peace. She keeps her cards pretty close to her chest." I remember how she paused before telling her story, maybe calculating what to say, how to tell us, and how much.

Francis gazes off to one side for a while, then back at me. "Claire, what I want you to know is, I may not have told you the whole truth all the time, but to the best of my ability I was straight with you, I tried to do right by you." We look at each other. "And I'm sorry if I scared you or upset you, or hurt you," he adds.

"I worried when you had those... episodes," I tell him.

"Yeah—the first one was the anniversary of Phoebe's death. Every year I sort of lose it around that time. The other time was on her birthday. Holidays weren't great, either. I could tell when one of those episodes was building, but there wasn't much I could do about it..." he shrugs.

"But you dumped me, Francis. You took off—" I pause, flooded by the memory of that day.

"Abandoned you?" he suggests.

I nod.

For a moment he's silent, then he says, "Remember how I used to charm everyone—everyone but you?"

"Yes."

"It wasn't that I couldn't," he says. "Only that I didn't. Remember old Jean, with the acanthus table? Lovely artifact, by the way. Do you recall that day?"

My cheek stings with the memory of it. The day it changed between us. "Yes."

"I did that on purpose."

I feel a surge of anger and hurt. "Why?"

He shakes his head. "Do you have any idea how young you were then, how gormless? You thought you were tough, but you weren't. You'd have done—you did do—whatever I asked you to. You trusted me too much. You were giving yourself away to me bit by bit. I needed you to hate me—" He holds up his right hand, index finger and thumb nearly touching, only the thickness of a matchstick between them "—just that much. I needed you to be angry at me. I needed us to be on opposite sides: you against me—or you were going to be a target for anyone like me, any sweet talker who came along. The Callums of the world. But I didn't want you too independent," he adds quickly. "Couldn't have you running off. But strangely enough, for my own sense of right and wrong, I needed you on your own team, not on mine. Did it work?"

"It did, yeah," I have to admit.

"Now," he says, then pauses for a beat, "who do you think called you out at the market?"

For a second the world freezes. My blood runs cold—I've read that phrase, and now I know what it feels like, ice starting at my centre and moving outward, numbing me. I recall the shout—a man's voice, loud, cutting through the mumbling murmur of conversations around me. I remember standing motionless, not even breathing, feeling the heavy thud, thud, thud of my heart in my chest, afraid that if I moved, I'd draw attention to myself, and the weight of all those people staring might crush me. At first, I tried to convince myself it wasn't me being called out. I'd lifted hundreds of objects and no one had ever noticed. I remember the dawning dread as I realized I'd been caught, and all eyes were on me.

I feel dizzy. For a second the breath is squeezed out of me. Then, in a low whisper, "You?" A wave of fury surges through me, red and hot.

"I had to. I did it to protect you."

"Oh, please. Give me a break." I spit the words out.

"The day at the market was when it all came clear to me. I saw we couldn't keep doing what we were doing any more. I'd known it for a while, but I'd been avoiding admitting it to myself. I kept telling myself lies, making excuses. Then, that day—I don't know why—it all stopped, I couldn't believe the lies anymore.

"I knew I needed to take off, but I wanted to leave you safe. I figured you'd be better off with other people than with me. Once you were gone, I could disappear. I assumed you'd get picked up by the cops or Children's Services."

Deryn starts to protest. He holds up his hand to stop her. "You were a minor," he tells me. "I was pretty certain they wouldn't throw the book at you—you hadn't done much bad. I figured they'd put you into the Youth Diversion system. Even if they sent you back to your Gran's, there'd be eyes on you. People would be looking out for you.

"It wasn't like I could go to the cops and come clean. What was I going to tell them? 'This young lady, officer? Well, yes, she's been travelling around with me; well, no, she's not my daughter, happens we're not related at all'—how do you think that would have played out? It would likely have played out with me in jail, and I'll be honest with you, I wasn't going to go to jail."

"You'll be honest with me?" I repeat, riding the wave of anger. "Eddy says you lied about the circus. You lie about everything."

A cryptic expression flickers across his face. "Not everything, surely. But I don't think it's a crime for me to tell you what I wanted to have happened instead of what actually happened—think of it as embroidering the truth. Does it really make so much difference how I ended up with the circus?"

"It makes it harder for me to believe you if I think you might be lying."

"Believe," he says the word lightly, with a hint of amusement. "Well, here's something for you to believe, I've never lied to you about what was important."

"Like what?" I demand. "How you said I reminded you of Phoebe? How, if she were on the street, you would have wanted someone to look out for her?"

He looks down and is quiet for a second, then he says in a low voice, "All that was true."

Maybe it's his tone—chastened, resigned, sad. My anger shrinks. He glances over. I meet his gaze. I think how he found me when I was lost and took me off the street, bought me meals when I was hungry, gave me boots and a coat against the winter cold, clean clothes, got me out of that situation with Callum. I remember how kind he could be—the teasing, the playfulness.

"You took good care of me," I allow. "You fed me and watched out for me. I was nervous about the stealing, angry the time you slapped me—" His eyes meet mine; his mouth tightens, he looks down "—but after a while I trusted you, mostly."

"Glad to hear it."

"And I learned a lot from you."

He looks skeptical. "I'm not sure what I gave you are what you'd call transferable life skills," he says.

"I think there may be applications," I say, glancing over at Deryn and Eddy, then back to Francis. "I'm starting to understand how they may be adaptable to many different situations."

"So," he says with an uneven grin, "I saved you, and you saved me."

"I saved you? How?"

"You trusted me," he says. "After a while. Despite everything. I'd fallen apart, to a degree, and you trusted me. I don't know, somehow it gave me ballast. Getting you off the street made me feel like I could. . .manage—but then the situation became more complicated.

"I figured out that to really deserve your trust, I had to let you go. I had to come up with a way to leave you, but do it safely. I'd always known the whole set-up was crazy. I engaged in what you might call magical thinking—if I could get you safe, it would all work out, but my solution wasn't really a solution after all, not a real, long-term one. In the end, what I did was equal parts inspired and desperate. But it was the best I could do at the time. Lucky for us, Derrie was there."

"Lucky for us," Deryn says, "Claire was paying attention."

"Francis," I say.

He looks at me, eyebrows raised. "Yes?"

"My knapsack," I say. "Where is it?"

"In the truck. Why?"

I look from him to Deryn, and back. I weigh how much to tell them. Everyone waits. "There's a picture of my mom in there," I tell him. "I want it back."

His expression softens. "Your mom."

"Yeah."

Then he smiles. "Well, you and Derrie turned out to be successful at finding lost people. There's another lost person we might go looking for. What do you say?"

I stare at him for a moment. "I have to think about it," I say finally.

"We should get going, Dad." She stands up and looks at Eddy. "Good to meet you again," she says.

He stands. "Good to meet you," he says. "Glad to see you all grown up."

She laughs shortly, then holds out her hand to Francis. "Come on, Dad."

We go downstairs, into the sunlight, Eddy, too.

Deryn says goodbye, then it's my turn. I feel awkward, unsure of what to say. "Thanks, Eddy."

"Any time," he tells me.

I wonder what comes next, where I'm going to go from here.

Francis and Deryn start to walk away. I stand, watching them go.

Deryn stops and turns around. "You coming?" She sounds impatient.

"Me?"

"You have somewhere else to go?" she asks. Knowing the answer, she turns and keeps walking. I weigh my options—go with them, or. . .? Then I remember the picture of my mother, and I hurry after them.

"He'll ride shotgun," Deryn says to me when I catch up. "You can sit in the middle."

When we get to the truck, she beeps the doors open and gets in. I climb in on the passenger side, scootch to the middle of the seat, Francis gets in after me.

I kneel on the seat and fish my knapsack out from the space behind it. I sit down, unzip the pocket, and pull out the photo. Francis leans sideways a bit. "I can see the resemblance," he says.

"Really?" I ask, looking up at him.

"Oh, sure," he says. "She looks like a firecracker, a real pistol."

Deryn says, "Home, Dad?"

He looks over at her and smiles. "Home," he says.

She looks at me. "We all good?"

I'm quiet for a second.

"We'll have to talk to your grandmother eventually," Deryn says, "sort it out with her, but we can do that later. Right now, I want to know you're sure you want to come with us."

I look at her, then Francis, then back to Deryn again. Is it what I want? I take a deep breath. This is as close to a family—sitting here between the two of them—as I've had in a long time. They feel more like family than Gran and I ever did. It might not work, but, as I'm sure Francis would point out if I put it to him, it might, and I won't know til I've tried. I decide to give it a go. After all, if there's anything I've learned from him, it's that if one scheme doesn't work out, there's always another opportunity around the next corner.

"We're all good," I say.

"Glad to hear it." Deryn nods. "Dad, we're going to get my car—it's just up the road. You're going to drive it, and I'm taking the truck."

"What? I have to drive that clunker?"

"Yes, you have to drive that clunker. I know you'll want your truck back. This way, I know you'll follow me home."

Francis sighs. "So young, and so cunning."

Deryn catches my eye. Hers are lit with laughter. "Learned from the best, Dad."

"So, Claire, lass," Francis says, leaning closer, his voice low and confiding in my ear, "about your mother—"

"Dad—" Deryn says sharply.

"Hear me out, Derrie," he says. "Just hear me out."

It's like a light switch has flipped on. He's back again—the old Francis, the Francis I rode all those country roads with.

I can feel his energy bubbling, his thoughts racing, plans unfurling. I look at Deryn. Our eyes meet. She grins, rolls her eyes, shakes her head. Then she turns the key in the ignition, the engine rumbles to life, she slips the truck into gear, and we head off.

Acknowledgements

Thanks as always to the home team: Don, Dugan & Kris & Lonan & Orrin, Hayden & Kim. I do not take your support for granted ever.

Thank you, Shelley Tanaka, for your insights and perspective about books, this book, the book world, and young people.

To Jane Warren, I am in your debt; your contributions are manifold, the book is immeasurably better because of them.

Thank you to Maureen Garvie, for your editorial insights and your calm, expert guidance.

Thanks are due to Susan Musgrave, for all sorts of *things* and *stuff*. Thank you for your acute editorial eye.

Thank you, as well, to the Inanna team: Evelyn Elgie and Melissa Ren. And for the beautiful cover, thank you to Juliane Van Huizen.

Thank you to the Ontario Arts Council for a Literary Creation Project Grant, which supported work on this novel, and to the City of Kingston Arts Fund (CKAF), and Kingston Arts Council for a Resiliency Grant received during work on this book.

Author

Melanie Dugan was born in San Francisco, California, and lived in London, England and Toronto before settling in Kingston, Ontario. She is the author of five novels, *Hard White* (". . .a very compelling and beautifully crafted story about an exceptional artist and I highly recommend it," *The Skeleton Press*), *Bee Summers* ("This is a coming-of-age novel that buzzes with intelligence and a deep understanding of human nature," Merilyn Simonds, author of *The Convict Lover*), *Dead Beautiful* ("A creative and reflective re-imagining of the Persephone myth, *Dead Beautiful* is a cheeky and thought-provoking romp through the Pantheon, the Underworld, and that peculiar little place called Earth that lies somewhere in between," Diane Schoemperlen, author of *Our Lady of the Lost and Found*.), *Revising Romance* ("heart-warming, amusing and . . . downright sexy," *Midwest Book* Review), and *Sometime Daughter* ("a stunning debut," *Kingston Whig-Standard*). Her short stories have been shortlisted for several awards, including the CBC Literary Award.

She has worked in many sectors of the book world: as Associate Publisher at Quarry Press, a publishing house in Kingston, Ontario; in several library systems; and in an independent bookstore. She worked as a publicist, and was promotions manager for the inaugural Kingston WritersFest.

An experienced public reader and speaker, Melanie has been featured in a variety of festivals and reading events, such as Word on the Street and the Prince Edward County Authors' Festival, as well as numerous benefit readings in Kingston.